THE RE

"DELPHI FABRICE" (the pseudo Adhémar Risselin, 1877-1937) began his career as an art critic with *Les Peintres de Bretagne* (1898), before becoming involved in the Decadent Movement, under the aesthetic of which he composed a number of works, including *L'Araignée rouge* (1903), the one-act drama *Clair de lune* (1903), which was co-written with Jean Lorrain, Fabrice's mentor, and *La sorcier rouge* (1910). Under the need for money, he gradually turned his attention romance novels, novels of adventure geared towards a juvenile audience, and "cine-novels" (adaptations of films into photo-novels). In all, he is credited with writing over 120 books.

BRIAN STABLEFORD'S scholarly work includes *New Atlantis: A Narrative History of Scientific Romance* (Wildside Press, 2016), *The Plurality of Imaginary Worlds: The Evolution of French roman scientifique* (Black Coat Press, 2017) and *Tales of Enchantment and Disenchantment: A History of Faerie* (Black Coat Press, 2019). In support of the latter projects he has translated more than a hundred volumes of *roman scientifique* and more than twenty volumes of *contes de fées* into English. His recent fiction, in the genre of metaphysical fantasy, includes a trilogy of novels set in West Wales, consisting of *Spirits of the Vasty Deep* (2018), *The Insubstantial Pageant* (2018) and *The Truths of Darkness* (2019), published by Snuggly Books, and a trilogy set in Paris and the south of France, consisting of *The Painter of Spirits*, *The Quiet Dead* and *Living with the Dead*, all published by Black Coat Press in 2019.

DELPHI FABRICE

THE RED SPIDER

TRANSLATED AND WITH AN INTRODUCTION BY

BRIAN STABLEFORD

THIS IS A SNUGGLY BOOK

Translation and Introduction Copyright © 2021 by
Brian Stableford.
All rights reserved.

ISBN: 978-1-64525-062-3

CONTENTS

Introduction / *7*

The Red Spider / *21*

Appendix: The Dedication / *197*

INTRODUCTION

L'ARAIGNÉE ROUGE by "Delphi Fabrice" (the pseudonym of Gaston-Henri-Adhémar Risselin, 1877-1937), herein translated as *The Red Spider*, was originally published in 1903 by Ambert et Cie. It was his first novel, but it remained his most famous, most of the hundred or so other novels he produced being rapidly forgotten. It had been preceded by a short play bearing the same title, scheduled to appear at La Scala theater in 1900 before the censor banned it—a prohibition that evidently caused the author considerable resentment, and was probably partly responsible for the deliberately scabrous nature of the novel extrapolated from the play. Extravagantly dedicated to Fabrice's flamboyant friend and mentor, Jean Lorrain, it can also be seen as a gesture of rebellious contempt addressed to the censorship that was striving in vain to hold back the tide of *fin-de-siècle* liberalism.[1]

The novel has retained a certain reputation as a horror story, and it was reprinted as such in 2004 by Terre

---

1 In the original book the dedicatory essay was placed, as usual, before the text, but it was presumably written afterwards, as a kind of explanatory footnote, and I have moved it to an appendix.

de Brume, along with the script of the play and other supplementary material, in a collection bearing the heading Terres Fantastiques, but its literary ancestry and context are considerably more complex, its primary affiliation being to the literary movement ironically labeled Decadent, which had found a significant early exemplar in Joris-Karl Husymans' novel *À rebours*, and of which Jean Lorrain had become the most prominent exponent and figurehead.

The Paris-born Delphi Fabrice launched his literary career as an art critic, his first book being *Les Peintres de Bretagne* (1898),[1] but he soon branched out into drama and short fiction. He had already formed a personal association with Jean Lorrain, who was a regular contributor of short fiction to *Le Journal*, then possessed of a stable of writers producing fiction or articles on a weekly or fortnightly basis, generally used as the lead items on page one; Lorrain mingled his admittedly fictional contributions with items that masqueraded as non-fiction, including a long-running social diary, signed "Raitif de la Bretonne" in honor of Nicolas Restif de La Bretonne's largely fictitious accounts of his supposed nocturnal wanderings in the city, collected as *Nuits de Paris* (1788-94). Fabrice copied his idol faithfully in his own regular contributions to the twice-weekly *Supplement* of the daily newspaper *La Lanterne* between 1902 and 1909, mingling orthodox

---

[1] Fabrice's family was presumably Breton in origin, but information on his background is very sparse; he apparently had a son, of whom there is no residual trace, but there is no evidence currently available via the internet regarding his private life; unusually, no portrait or photograph of him appears to have survived.

fiction with items of fake autobiography and social gossip, some of which were collected in his curious journalistic account of *L'Opium à Paris* (1907), the most successful of his "non-fiction" books. The *Supplement* reprinted much of the text of *L'Araignée rouge*, piecemeal, as "Pages retrouvées" in 1908. Fabrice also worked in association with Lorrain's friend Oscar Méténier, who founded the Grand-Guignol theater in 1897, but continued to support and supply material to other theaters, collaborating with him on various dramatic projects.

By the time of Jean Lorrain's death in 1906, Fabrice's career had diversified considerably. In 1904 he began to produce comedies based on works written for children a century before by the Comtesse de Ségur, and much of his subsequent work was aimed at a similar audience; he eventually became a prolific writer of action-adventure novels that would have been called "boys' books" had they been written in English. Following an inevitable deflection by the Great War of 1914-18, he did return to his work as a chronicler of the seamier side of Parisian life for a further decade, but in a relatively desultory fashion; his action-adventure novels came far more to the fore in the final years of his life, when he also produced illustrated film novelizations. The full extent of Fabrice's editorial work is unknown, but he might well have been on the staff of *La Lanterne* while he was publishing prolifically in the *Supplement*, and he was also on the staff of *Gil Blas* for a while. The extent of his ghost-writing is similarly unrecorded, although he is widely assumed to have helped Jean Lorrain out when the latter had trouble meeting his deadlines, especially after Lorrain moved to

Nice in 1900 for health reasons, only visiting Paris at intervals thereafter.

The probability that Fabrice did some ghost-writing for other people associated with Lorrain is particularly intriguing with regard to Liane de Pougy (1869-1950), to whom he often dedicated work and with whom he worked on several acknowledged collaborations. Pougy's career as a prominent "courtesan" was planned and guided by the self-styled Comtesse Valtesse de la Bigne, who had aided her own quest to add a touch of class to her career as a pretentious prostitute by publishing a quasi-autobiographical novel, and she advised Pougy to do the same. Pougy would undoubtedly have turned initially to Lorrain for help, as he was playing a leading role in supplying her publicity in the newspapers, but it is highly likely that the ever-busy Lorrain delegated the task to Fabrice, who might well have made a substantial contribution to the novels *L'Insaissable* (1898) and *Myrrhille* (1899), the subject-matter of which is echoed in several "courtesan novels" bearing his own signature.

Of particular relevance to the present volume is the fact that Lorrain, having charged himself with writing a ballet for Pougy, who was not a good dancer, came up with the idea of writing a leading part for her in which she hardly had to move, merely exhibiting herself in a gaudily flimsy costume, masquerading as a spider lying in wait in its web while the members of the chorus, playing her prospective prey, did most of the actual dancing. The ballet, *L'Araignée d'or* [The Golden Spider], was staged at the Folies Bergère in 1896 and caused something of a sensation. Fabrice was not the only writer to take some influence from it in deploying a similar symbolism.

The dramatic version of *L'Araignée rouge* scheduled for production in 1900 was not so extravagant, and the symbolic spider is modestly incarnated therein as a ring worn by the principal male character, whose sinister mien alarms a group of prostitutes, although Lili Mamour consents, reluctantly, to let him buy her dinner, when she is surprised that he takes no food himself, and also refuses to kiss her. She refuses to put on the spider ring when he asks her to do so, or to touch the hand on which he wears it, and when he takes out a box containing a real spider she panics and calls for help—which, when it arrives, causes the man to withdraw, enigmatically and anticlimactically. The lead part was scheduled to be played by another of Lorrain's protégées, the music hall performer Polaire (Émilie-Marie Bouchard, 1874-1939), who subsequently had a breakthrough in her career in 1902, when she played the part of Claudine in a successful stage adaptation of Colette's novels—which were then still credited to Willy, the author's husband—and who eventually became a star of silent movies. When the novel *L'Araignée rouge* was published, Fabrice got Polaire—to whom Lorrain used to refer affectionately as "La Cantharide d'or" [golden "Spanish fly"]—to write a review of it for the *Lanterne Supplement*, which appeared above the latest episode of the current Claudine feuilleton.

Symbolic spiders were not new to the Decadent Movement in 1898, of course, and one particularly significant example, Marcel Schwob's "Arachné," had been published in 1889 in the *Écho de Paris*, shortly before Lorrain joined the stable of writers producing fiction regularly for that newspaper, prior to shifting his allegiance to *Le Journal*. Like Fabrice's novel, Schwob's story is a vivid account of hallucination, in which a young man who murders his mistress out of jealousy imagines her enjoying a strange afterlife as the goddess Arachne, who will soon suck him dry of all life and bear his ingested spirit away through the Realm of the Spiders to a paradise of amour—an optimism that the reader is not encouraged to share. Fabrice's similar evocation of Arachne might, of course, be coincidental, but whether or not that is the case, there is a crucial difference in the symbolism of the two stories, arising from the fact that the protagonist of Schwob's story is obviously heterosexual whereas the protagonist of Fabrice's is equally obviously, and crucially, not.

There is an inevitably-strong temptation to regard the protagonist of Fabrice's novel as a transfiguration of Jean Lorrain and to decode the plot as a narrative of psychological panic induced by reluctant homosexuality. The treatment of homosexual desire and responses to it in Lorrain's own fiction, which evolved considerably in the course of his career, lends considerable support to the hypothesis that his own homosexuality, initially masked by his dandyism and his fascination with the young women whose careers he promoted enthusiastically in his journalism, but increasingly obvious to his literary and theatrical acquaintances before becoming publicly notorious in the late 1890s, was something with which he struggled. His fiction often represents veiled and unacknowledged homosexual desire as a kind of dangerous occult fascination, and it is very easy indeed to read *L'Araignée rouge* in a similar way. It is probably a drastic oversimplification, however, to construe the novel's protagonist, Andhré, simply as a disguised representation of Lorrain. There are certainly many aspects of his biography that contrast sharply with Lorrain's as well as a few that reflect it, and the assimilation leaves open and enigmatic the question of exactly where the author fits into the picture. It is worth taking note that Jean Lorrain does not seem to have taken offense at the characterization of Andhré, as he would have been fully entitled to do had he construed it to be a depiction of him.

It is also worth noting in this context that another novel published in 1903. *Les Androgynes,* by Jane de La Vaudère, contains a much more blatant and extremely unflattering depiction of Lorrain, as the writer Jacques Chozelle, who adopts a younger writer, André, as his protégé, partly in order to exploit him as a ghost-writer but also with the intention of corrupting him by drawing him into an underworld of secret homosexual orgies and opium smoking. Chozelle has written a ballet for a dancer named Tigrane in which she plays a giant spider, which is described in sufficient detail to make it perfectly obvious that the work the author has in mind is *L'Araignée d'or.* Tigrane had previously featured briefly in "L'Hippique" (1899; tr. as "The Horse-Show")—one of La Vaudère's newspaper stories written for *La Presse*, in the same subgenre as Lorrain's fiction for *Le Journal*—in which she is an ambitious courtesan trying to inveigle an artist to paint a portrait of her that will depict her as a green spider: "a monster and a rare jewel, a prodigious, divine and terrible monster." The two works leave no doubt that

Tigrane is a transfiguration of Liane de Pougy, but it is not so easy to form a definite judgment to whether the André of *Les Androgynes* is a disguised representation of Delphi Fabrice.

Jane de La Vaudère would surely have been acquainted with Fabrice, because the two of them both collaborated with Oscar Méténier in the late 1890s. Furthermore, there are strong affinities between La Vaudère's work for *La Presse* in 1898-1901 and the series of stories that Fabrice published under the heading "Fleurs d'Éther et de Talus"[1] in the *Lanterne Supplement* in 1903. Although the affinities could be the simple result of similar interests, it is tempting to wonder whether Fabrice might have had a hand in such fairground-set stories as "Lapins de bois" (1899; tr. as "Wooden Rabbits"), and whether his suggestions might have been the source of the depictions of the episodes in *Les Androgynes* set in the Parisian homosexual underworld.[2] It is also possible that their acquaintance

---

1 The "talus" [slope] to which this title refers euphemistically is the remains of the old fortifications of Paris, which Lorrain and Fabrice referred to familiarly in their journalism and fiction as the "fortifs," the ditches of which had become a favorite location of Parisian sexual encounters in the late 1890s, employed by legions of prostitutes of both sexes.

2 The detailed description of the party to which Chozelle takes André as the first step in his corruption might be based on newspaper reportage; in was also in 1903 that a scandal broke in the newspapers regarding "living tableaux" of ephebes exhibited during parties hosted by the writer Jacques d'Adelswärd-Fersen (1880-1923), who was eventually hounded out of Paris and was subsequently resident in Capri. Lorrain had met his fellow dandy Adelswärd-Fersen in Venice in 1902, and was surely on his guest list; he is featured in the latter's *roman à clef Lord Lyllian* (1905), but as to whether Fabrice ever accompanied Lorrain to one of his friend's parties we can only speculate.

was not entirely harmonious, as the eventual fate of André in *Les Androgynes* is not so very different from the fate of Andhré in *L'Araignée rouge*. The fact that one of the prostitutes in the dramatic version of *L'Araignée rouge* is named Jane du Val-Noble might be of no significance at all, but it is a curious choice.

The situation is further complicated by the fact that Jean Lorrain also published a story entitled "L'Araignée rouge" in January 1903, immediately prior to the publication of Fabrice's book, in a sequence headed "Femmes" in *Le Journal*. In Lorrain's story, the eponymous symbol features in a painting of a comtesse whose death, occasioned by abuse of chloroform, might or might not be accidental. The sequence of scathing character studies bearing the heading "Femmes" includes an extremely catty depiction of "Illyne Yls," an actress clearly based on Liane de Pougy, and although she does not seem to have reacted angrily, another of Lorrain's former protégées, the artist Jeanne Jacquemin, took legal action against him for his use of details of her life and career in "Victime," published less than a month later,[1] resulting in a conviction and an award of absurdly high punitive damages, which were only overturned on appeal in October 1903 because Jacquemin relented in her pursuit. That prosecution, as well as the publicity associated with the prosecution of Jacques d'Adelswärd-Fersen in the same year, had a drastic

---

1 "Victime" is translated as "Victim" in an appendix to the Lorrain collection *Fards and Poisons* (2019), which also contains translations of "Illyne Yls" and "L'Araignée rouge," the latter run together with the previous item in the "Femmes" series, as it had been in the French version of the collection, *Fards et Poisons* (1903), as "Monsieur Smith."

cooling effect on the overlapping fiction and society gossip featured in Lorrain's and Fabrice's newspaper columns, the editors of which became far more risk-sensitive.

Given all these incidental details, the context in which Fabrice's novel was produced was itself a strange and intricate web, which does not help to make the calculatedly-enigmatic novel any easier to interpret, or the author's elusive rhetorical stance any easier to evaluate. The novel's notional narrator poses as a user of both ether and morphine, just as "Delphi Fabrice" does in the "Fleurs d'Éther et de Talus" series—prompting Polaire to begin her solicited review of the text with a cautionary insistence that she was neither a writer nor a morphine addict—but it would be a mistake to assume that the actual Fabrice had the same vices to the same extent. By the time Lorrain wrote his notorious *contes d'un buveur d'éther* he had given up using the stimulant, and he was by no means the only writer to make use of exaggerated publicity of his former drug abuse in order to support and cement his reputation for "decadence." By the time the two writers met, Lorrain was aware that the after-effects of his previous ether abuse were slowly killing him, and he began referring to himself as "Le Cadavre" long before it completed its work; the example that he provided for his young acolyte might, therefore, have been salutary rather than corrupting, whatever impression Jane de La Vaudère might have formed of his relationships. For connoisseurs of Decadent fiction, however, such complications can only add to the fascination of the text.

L'Araignée rouge does deserve its reputation as a horror story, and is likely to please fans of horror fiction, who can consider it as a significant contribution to the rich tradition of graphic literary accounts of descents into lurid madness. It is also, however, a deliberate attempt to take the notion of Baudelairean *spleen de Paris*—the pathological extrapolation of a particular modern species of existential *ennui*—to a new extreme. That was not an easy task, as it had previously been tackled by writers of great ability in landmark works, Jean Lorrain's story-series "Astarté," reprinted in book form as *Monsieur de Phocas* (1900), being a conscious attempt to exceed Joris-Karl Huysmans' already-excessive *À rebours*. Perhaps Fabrice was aiming to vault a bar set too high, or at least arriving in the arena belatedly, but *L'Araignée rouge* was certainly a bold attempt to fulfill its purpose, deserving of respect and admiration; its translation into English is perhaps long overdue, although, as with many other risqué French works, it could not possibly have been published legally in England or America at the time of its first appearance, or for at least half a century thereafter.

The translation was made from a copy of the 2004 Terre de Brume edition kindly supplied by the publisher at the time of its publication. The heavy use of Parisian argot in some chapters made this translation difficult, even with the assistance of Bob, the standard dictionary of such argot, and the relative mildness of equivalent terms in an Anglo-American idiom inevitably deprives the account of a little of its spice, but I have done my best to preserve the meaning and the implication.

—Brian Stableford, August 2020.

THE RED SPIDER

IT was about ten years ago that I met Andhré Mordann, ten years during which, at the hazard of our meetings in Paris and in the Guérandaise peninsula in Bretagne, we lived side by side for two or three days at a time, with the fine facility that young men have for linking themselves together and separating in the same way.

I saw him for the first time in Nantes,[1] a city of good life and sweet pleasure, on an evening spent idling in the sailors' quarter. An inn parasite—a Pantinoise become Nantaise, God alone knows after what adventures— had brought us together. With our elbows on the table, dragging out three glasses of tafia, we had chatted about everything and nothing: the sensations that life procures, art and ennui, all in blond tobacco smoke, mingled with ludicrous reflections on the clients of the hospitable dive.

The Pantinoise did not take long to abandon our society, having sensed that there was nothing doing. We

---

1 Exactly when and where Delphi Fabrice first met Jean Lorrain is not recorded, but given Fabrice's evident fondness for Bretagne and Jean Lorrain's well-documented love of seaports it would not be surprising if the encounter had taken place is some such location.

were not drinkers and the hussy, a flower of the Parisian fortifications, habituated at a young age to alcohol, appeared to be fond of tafia. She joined a group of sailors at the far end of the room, who were gesticulating, howling, singing and consuming three months' pay as only seamen know how to consume three months' pay in one night.

> *The lad has shown his bowsprit,*
> *The lad has shown his bowsprit,*
> *And the lass has fallen for*
> *My jolly pink heart*
> *My jolly rose-bush heart!*

And the sailors laughed and repeated in chorus:

> *My jolly pink heart*
> *My jolly rose-bush heart!*

That racket amused us a little, but at length we wearied of it and we left the concert. Wandering this way and that along the Rue des Marins and the Rue des Trois-Matelots throughout the quarter of maritime amour and the Quai de la Fosse, bizarre and picturesque Old Nantes, visiting taverns offering *gros plant* wine and glasses of tafia to all the belated wanderers of the port, we only went back to our respective hotels at first light. The next day we met up again and lived the same existence, the same good-humored debauchery that seaports offer. That same evening, he left.

Thereafter, as I said, at each of our encounters we resumed a common existence, both as avid for new visions, refined sensations in incessantly changing environments. A good companion, having original observations and particular judgments to make on all things, he pleased me, although I found his manner a little strange, a little mysterious, and even flashy, because of the bizarre rings ornamented with large gemstones that circled his fingers.

Mysterious? In truth, yes, his manner seemed mysterious to me, from the very first evening, the evening when we met.

Along the narrow and tortuous Rue des Marins, which descends so steeply toward the quay, all drinking dens, pot-bellied houses and buildings with prognathous ground floors, if I might put it thus, with barred windows capriciously distributed over the facades and massive doors pierced by judas-holes, low scary houses that reek of fever, he walked at a stealthy pace, and I had compared him to one of those figures painted by the Clouets, or Louis Balzac d'Entragues,[1] in the minor halls of the Louvre, especially. Yes, he realized very well the type of the seigneurs attached to the last Valois, with bony faces elongated by a fine beard, with thin lips, steely eyes and a cruelly cold physiognomy, with a defiant gait, the gestures of a fencer ever-ready for a feint and riposte, and a cunning mind. Andhré's eyes, above all, disconcerted me: steely blue eyes that gave him a fixed and fascinating gaze beneath the eternal soft felt hat he wore. That gaze

---

1 Louis de Balzac Illiers d'Entragues (1664-1720) was a prominent prelate who became a convert to Jansenism. Jean and François Clouet were sixteenth-century painters primarily known for portraits of members of the ruling family.

intimidated me when we first met, but the embarrassment soon disappeared; my friend was so amiable. And then, his bizarre eyes were only one more originality of his original person—for my friend Andhré Mordann was an eccentric.

It was only on the days after his departures that my curiosity awoke. Where did he come from? Whence came the money that he spent recklessly, without counting it? What about his family, his friends? In sum, who was the individual who existed for me under the named Andhré Mordann, a name that seemed to have escaped from a tale of korrigans? For several days those nagging questions were posed in my mind, and I promised myself to ask him next time I encountered him.

Oh, I would resolve the enigma! I would know . . . but then my thought flew elsewhere, my imagination bestrode the hippogriff of literature, and the memory of Andhré Mordann became imprecise, fading away again into the mist. And when the man emerged from who knows where, at a street corner, when I perceived him there before me, his hand extended—his long-fingered, mobile hand laden with rings, a hand that seemed to have a life independent of the individual—under the strangeness of the eyes of steel, the interrogation stopped on my lips. I abandoned my hand, smiling; and less than two minutes thereafter, my apprehensions forgotten and vanished, I was walking on his arm, gripped again by the magic of our special amity.

And there were one, two or three days of indescribable joys.[1]

---

1 In 1901, when Fabrice was presumably writing *L'Araignée rouge*, his meetings with Lorrain must have become intermittent, restricted

Oh, the evenings spent together, the very short, very sweet and very dear evenings, in the décor of the Paris boulevardier, of art exhibitions and theatrical premières, the décor of Paris in fête, blinding with raw light, intoxicating with noise and consented kisses, evenings at Maxim's and evenings in the worst faubourgs eaten by darkness: Grenelle, the Point-du-jour and the Place d'Italie—and also exquisite evenings in Bretagne, near Guérande-la-Figée, in the sad peace of sleepy little Breton ports under the golden eye of the Moon, on the solitary road, so desolate and so melancholy, that links Le Pouliguen, the burg of Batz and Le Croisic via the misty salt-marshes. We no longer quit one another. I was enthusiastic about everything and about nothing, about fragile Parisian orchids, the mask of a lover of the waste ground or the water's edge, the silhouette of a fresh-skinned sailor emerging from the shadows. He held himself in reserve, smiling discreetly. Only at the moment of pleasure—rarely—did his hands perform particular somersaults.

Then, one morning, that fraternal existence ceased. Abruptly, without a reason, he came to me in traveling costume, and shook my hand with a grip so strong that his rings encrusted stigmata in my flesh. In the shadow of his lowered felt hat, for a second, his eyes were stained with silver.

I encountered him for the last time five months ago.

It was in Paris, in the beautiful Parisian September, on the Quai Voltaire. Once more the questions vanished from my lips; I abandoned myself to his arms. We ran all

---

to the latter's brief returns to Paris from Nice; on such occasions, Lorrain usually stayed at a hotel on the Quai Voltaire.

day from bookshops to print merchants, and ended up purchasing two Japanese albums, two albums of Hokusai, in a perfect state in sheets of rice paper, on which extended, convulsively, the long thin flexible legs of spiders with bright multicolored bodies and ferocious eyes.

"Admirable, these albums, don't you think?" he said to me when we emerged from the bookshop and walked along the quay in the shade of bronzed trees, beside the Seine, which reflected the joy of the azure, scaled with silver by the passage of the *bateaux-mouches* and lighters. "Have you noticed the fantastic aspect that Hokusai's spiders have and the contrast between the large, obese bodies stuffed with blood and health of all those cut-throats, all those bloodsuckers, and the slender, exhausted legs, which seek prey to nourish the gaping belly? Oh, those Japanese spiders, how well they lie in ambush in their webs, and how one senses that they are about to pounce on you! And what a desire for carnage there is in those watchful eyes?"

At the same time, Andhré opened one of the albums, indicating a plate in which a lurking spider was observing a fly approaching the trap.

"What am I saying? More than the desire for carnage; can you not read in those eyes a ferocious lust that is about to be satisfied, which cannot be satisfied?"

He interrupted himself; his hands somersaulting. Then he continued, laughing:

"What a joy for me, the discovery of these albums!"

In the evening, sickened, after wandering through a fairground in Vaugirard, a fair in which the beautiful Fatmas were, in order not to change, former milliners from Batignolles, wrestlers, unemployed butcher-boys and animal tamers—

Molded, braced, costumed in deerskin.
Flexing thighs and backs

as I no longer know what amorphous poet says—tamers who were ex-café-concert bouncers, we took refuge in a bar in the Rue Royale. Slightly weary, we were no longer talking. We were sucking crayfish when I thought I saw, running over one of his fingers, a large brown spider with a shiny body, as shiny as a red pearl.

I jumped, for the sight of a spider has always filled me with horror and disgust

Andhré saw my movement, recoiled slightly, and said, smiling: "Don't move. It's a ring, dear friend, a simple ring. Marvelously executed, isn't it? A masterpiece, a pure masterpiece, signed Charles de Monvel."[1]

He had removed the ring from his finger, and, after having handled it voluptuously for some time, he placed it on the table. The insect seemed thus to be set at the tip of an invisible thread. I was alarmed before that representation of a spider, an ornament that only a sick mind could have conceived.

I looked at Andhré. He was troubled. His eyes, his steely eyes, were more stained with white than ever. And

---

1 Charles Boutet de Monvel (1855-1913) was a significant practitioner of "art nouveau." His famous "bat-maiden" ring (1900) had recently been exhibited when the novel was published. He also designed a notable "serpent ring" but the spider ring is an invention.

his hands! They were trembling, leaping; the fingers seemed to elongate and become contorted.

Then an unknown courage came to me. I leaned toward him and, with my face close to his, my eyes gazing into his, the question—the nagging question that had been tormenting me for so many years, emerged like a cry . . .

"In sum, who are you? Tell me, tell me . . . who are you?"

His eyes became bluer, a deep sapphire hue. The shuddering of his hands stopped. Abruptly, his entire person froze.

Then, with a slow gesture, he replaced the ring on his finger. And without a word, without looking at me, and before, mute with surprise, I could make the slightest movement to retain him, he went to the door and disappeared into a group that was leaving.

Five minutes later I was on the sidewalk of the Rue Royale searching for my friend—but alas, he was not among the figures who were passing by or drawing away.

I was never to see him again.

One evening, however, on returning to Paris from a voyage to Flanders—black and white Flanders, of a white that is not white and a black that is not black—I chanced to go into a café near the prefecture of police: a café where the reporters of all the newspapers met to exchange information about the latest crime, the latest judiciary affair with which the court was dealing.

I was alone in a corner, glad to be in Paris again, with its busy atmosphere and pleasant speech, smoking a hasty cigarette of blond tobacco, trying to extract a little parisianism from the ambient gaiety, when a name was suddenly uttered:

"Andhré Mordann . . ."

Andhré Mordann, someone had said, Andhré Mordann . . . My throat contacted. An indescribable emotion gripped me. I approached the group from which the name had been launched. I listened breathlessly, while around me the reporters took notes on what one of them was saying—a fat man (I can still see him) uttering brief sentences between two swigs of beer.

"This morning, at ten o'clock, while making their round, two wardens of the Montparnasse cemetery perceived a man covered in blood hiding among the tombstones. As they approached, the individual tried to flee, but, devoid of strength, he could not put his project into execution. The guards tried to take the unknown man to the bureau in order to lavish the care upon him that his condition demanded and to interrogate him regarding the reasons for his presence in the necropolis, but they were obliged to undertake a fierce struggle. The man, grinding his teeth, his eyes bulging, clung on to the tombstones. It required four more wardens to reckon with the maniac and they literally had to carry him. The unknown man only uttered a single cry: 'Her . . . ! Her . . . !'[1]

---

1 French pronouns do not work in the same way as English ones, so the "elle," in the original version would not necessarily mean "her" rather than "it," if it were referring to a non-human entity described by a noun with a female gender, such as *araignée*. Subsequently, whenever Andhré refers to his imaginary haunter as "*le fantôme*," he naturally uses the pronoun *il*, which I have translated as "it," but I thought it more appropriate to use "her" at this point and in certain other places.

"Various papers found in his pockets permitted his identity to be ascertained. He was one Andhré Mordann, of an excellent family, resident in Paris in the boulevard ***. The unfortunate, approximately thirty years old, had been afflicted by mental alienation, and it is doubtless in the course of a crisis that, favored by the night, he had scaled the cemetery wall.

"Andhré Mordann, whose family has been informed, was taken to the special infirmary of the Dépôt, on the instructions of the police commissaire of the quarter."

Mad! He was mad! But maddened by what? By Her, the Her to whom he was appealing, from whom he perhaps awaited help . . . but who was she?

That tortured me as I returned home. In vain I remained in the journalists' café for two hours, hoping that further details might be given, but nothing came; the name of Andhré Mordann was not even pronounced again. And I left, disappointed.

I wanted to know, to know that lugubrious tragedy in its entirety—for tragedy there was. I scarcely suspected the elements of it. A thirst for truth rose within me and tortured me. I could seek information at the prefecture—someone there would have talked to me about the lugubrious story—but no; the police would know nothing. They would only know the precise fact that had necessitated my poor friend's internment. Oh yes, he was my friend, was he not? For he still was; I felt it, and that in spite of our quarrel, beyond it. Yes, I had the sentiment that our bizarre amity had survived.

What if I were to present myself at his home, I thought? But no. I was afraid of the house, which must be hallucinating in its abandonment. And then, perhaps I would find his family there, since it had been said that he had a family. How could I explain myself to people in tears, overwhelmed by the loss of a dear being? How could I tell them about my relationship with Andhré, our strange liaison—and also the scene, the last scene in the café in the Rue Royale? No, I could do nothing in order to know; I had to keep silent, to remain in uncertainty and indecision.

My slumber was populated by frightful nightmares. I saw Andhré again, an Andhré whose steely eyes had become dead water, an Andhré whose hands, the hands that had always obsessed me, were convulsive, whose fingers were agitating like the tentacles of a squid. He was smiling at me, with his discreet and sad smile . . . And abruptly, the figure loomed up beside him of an apocalyptic beast, a Medusa whose hair slowly enlaced my friend and made him disappear, absorbing him in a thicket of vipers.

In the morning, having risen early, I ran to the nearest newspaper kiosk and collected all the papers. But all of them only repeated the banal text that had been repeated before me the previous day; and I returned home furious, crumpling the gazettes.

Oh, that whole day of agitation, the exacerbation of my nerves, which I could not calm by reading, walking, or even an opiate preparation! The memory of Andhré Mordann, our walks, our final encounter, and the madness of the unfortunate . . . an entire phantasmagoria hatched from our tremulous hearts like a vacillating night-light, the last sparks of which played on the membranous wings of a chimera of anguish that I sensed, crouching and hypnotic, nearby . . .

Toward evening, when I began to calm down, my domestic came to tell me that the concierge wanted to speak to me. Enervated, I was about to send the man to the devil when he opened the door and came in.

"Excuse me, Monsieur," he said, "but we're afraid . . . with regard to what has been deposited so oddly . . . it put us in suspicion . . . We dared not give it to Monsieur . . . we were waiting for Monsieur to mention it . . . but since Monsieur is agitated today . . . we thought, my wife and I, that it was perhaps for the thing . . . So, here it is, Monsieur . . . Monsieur will excuse us . . . we thought it was the right thing to do . . ."

And the fellow handed me a packet.

Feverishly, I opened it. It contained a little oak-wood box, a Breton box of sixteenth-century workmanship, with rose designs, garlands and figures carved in the wood. I recognized it immediately. Andhré had acquired it in my presence, in the early days of our relationship. Yes, it really was the box that he had unearthed in the home of a worker in the salt-marshes, at Kervalet, a little lost village in the vicinity of Batz, one afternoon of random roaming.

My heart leapt in my breast.

"Ah," the concierge continued, "there was also an envelope for Monsieur . . ."

I read these simple scrawled words—veritable "spider-legs":

> *My friend, examine these papers.*
> *Her! Her!*
> *You shall know.*
>   *Andhré.*

While I rummaged in the box and assembled these pages of ancient and recent handwriting, I learned that during the night, a man had deposited at the door of the concierge's lodge an envelope and a packet. The next day—which is to say, the same day—on unwrapping the parcel and the missive, the concierge had feared a trick. He had resolved not to hand me anything unless I asked for it, until, after a week, he would inform me or my domestic. It was only on learning of my state of nervousness that they decided to give me the singular dispatch, suspecting that there might be some correlation between my malaise and those things.

I read Andhré's alarming, sinister confession, simultaneously sensual and chaste, traced with an extraordinary clarity, as cold as the gaze of his eyes of steel, thoughts as insidious and guileful as his elegant feline manner, his portrait descended from a Clouet portrait.

And here they are, these pages of anguish and extravagance, here is this ridiculous and yet real suffering, faithfully transcribed. I have not changed a word or deformed a phrase, for I am one of those who think that in "arranging" memoirs, journals of intimate life, one always deranges them considerably.

Here they are with their madness and their sincerity—reflections of a calm and anxious, great and puerile soul, the soul of a giant, the soul of a puppet, who descended into infernal circles even lower than the those of the old Florentine poet . . . yes, even lower than the region of unnamed dolors, into the bloody darkness from which even the red legion of demons flees in terror, like a stampede . . .

I

"ANDHRÉ... I'm ready... are you coming?"

It is Louisette, my little cousin Louisette, my childhood companion and future wife, who is calling me, sending me that invitation to go for a walk through my bedroom door.

Yes, I'm ready, and have been for two hours. For two hours I've been going back and forth, like a wild beast in its cage. I'm so bored I could cry—oh, stupidly, without really knowing why. And yet nothing here is disagreeable or antipathetic. From the window I can see the most enchanting of landscapes extending: in the distance, pink and blue hills that festoon the horizon capriciously; then the black masses of the forest of Compiègne; villages that are bright patches; meadows, fields of gold, crimson and tender green; and, nearer, the edge of the wood of Là-Haut, the Carlepontais wood with enamored foliage; the village of Carlepont, a picturesque accumulation of blue-scaled slates and red tiles corroded by moss, descending all the way to the road, and over which the sun causes golden cascades to pour, which continue streaming in the sand of the path.

Oh, I'm bored!

It isn't Paris that I miss; I have no nostalgia for the theaters and music halls, the racecourses and the picturesque and literary salons, amorous ladies devoid of youth, night cafés, excursions into all the corners of public and private Pleasure of the great city. I'm cured of the stupid sensations that one feels so scantly or feels too much in which the contemporary mind completes itself I've lived all those things very rapidly, perhaps too rapidly. That's why I'm so bored, why my pointless youth is adrift. I'm uncertain in confrontation with uncertainty.

For three months that torpor has held me under its spell and exacerbated without my mind—although it would have liked to do it—acquiring enough strength to pull itself together.

Yes, three months ago, in Paris, in our large family residence lost on the bank of the Bièvre, I was wandering from room to room, dragging my idleness from the main drawing room to the boudoir where my mother and my cousin were spending hours of activity poring over their tapestries.

"I'm weary of being weary," I replied to the good Doctor de Fauvières, from whom my anxious mother wanted to discover the causes of my strangeness. And the next day we left for our property in Carlepont. I sensed in the suddenness of that resolution the influence of Doctor de Fauvières' advice. It did not annoy me. Are not being bored in Paris and being bored in the country still being bored?

"Andhré! Are you coming, then?"

It's the impatient voice of Louisette that rises in the soothing silence. Poor Louisette! Poor little cousin! Well, no, I'm not coming. A walk in the wood has no charm for me. For a week now, under the pretext of distracting me, I've been forced to stroll in the greenery, which irritates me with its monotony and its stony paths. No, I'm not coming. I've had enough of the country—enough!

Scarcely have I proffered those words than I hear Louisette's footsteps drawing away, as if regretfully. She doesn't want to annoy me, the dear child. At the risk of attracting an observation from Maman, who must have charged her with bringing me, no matter what the cost, she is going away, alone.

And, sprawled on a chaise longue, I lose myself in the ocean of my thoughts. I resuscitate the past.

My childhood was unhealthy, Fevers, especially the redoubtable typhoid, assailed it. At the age of ten I was puny and debilitated, so puny that I appeared to be little more than six years old, so puny that my intellectual faculties were deplorable. My thoughts had no impetus; I did not fatigue anyone with my tyrannical childish babble; my brain was only slumbering, the pure slumber of death. Only my mask of suffering, my drawn and wan features, the indelible marks that the malady leaves on those who have experienced it, testified to my age, perhaps already making me old.

At school I was an indolent, dismal pupil afflicted by sloth, the cancer that professors execrate, of which the skepticism of student teachers complain, and which is disdained by the conceit of every "academically strong" scholar. My family shared all those sentiments in my regard. So when, shortly after scraping through my baccalaureate, I announced my intention to devote myself to literature, there was only one cry of disapproval. Not that my father, a former officer who had fought in the wars under the Second Empire, execrated "letters," but for him, that career was not and could not be mine. In his mind, a litterateur was a sort of Quixotic poseur, exuberant, maddening and mad, an individual of scandalous and controversial exterior. For three months he heaped me with sermons and remonstrations, expressing unreservedly, without even thinking that it might offend me, how conscious he was of my mediocrity, a mediocrity that could only find employment by . . . wearing the epaulette![1]

I held firm, clinging stubbornly to my project—without discussion, it goes without saying. No one else in my position would have had such superb arrogance. They would have screamed or sobbed, taking heaven as their witness of the sincerity of their vocation; but that was not in my temperament. I opposed mutism, a more powerful argument than any wrath—and my apathy triumphed.

Before the impotence of their efforts, my family left me tranquil. Perhaps they thought that I would be quickly discouraged when I had understood my absolute lack of talent. Hence, they abandoned me. I lived as I wished; I became even more somber and more taciturn. Soon, society horrified me, and I became a misanthrope. I shut myself in my room for entire days, avoiding showing myself in the house.

---

1 This bears no resemblance to Jean Lorrain's biography; as to whether or not it might reflect Fabrice's, we can only speculate, but Fabrice did write a few sardonic works with a military backcloth.

My mother and my older sister, very active in social life, only thinking about soirées and receptions, dresses and hairstyles, felt embarrassed by my presence. For them I was a bird of ill-omen, a hindrance, a morose spirit whose face rendered speech refractory to the appeals of joy. They set up camp in the drawing room, a room into which I only penetrated rarely, when imperious necessity constrained me to do so. My father, a brave soldier who only dreamed of revenge, gradually became disinterested in an "accursed idle dreamer."

I had a clear perception of all that: the ill-humor of my mother and my sister, the discontentment of my father, and even the sly scorn of the servants.

Because of my myopia, the army did not take me. My family, deciding then that there was definitely nothing to be done with me, made the decision to give me the cold shoulder, to set me completely aside. They only tolerated my presence because they thought that I was incapable of earning a living—"for the honor of a name that has never been tarnished," my father muttered.

Thus my existence continued: a boat descending a river at the whim of the current, always solitary, naked and indifferent in the midst of a general indifference.

I did very little work, only writing in rare hours of extreme idleness, when I felt truly too weary. What I wrote then were thin studies of a special psychology, of a character so particular that a generalization, even with two or three broadly similar cases, was almost impossible. The characters and entities that I created remained unique in unique frames. Thus composed, my literature might have been interesting and original if I had had a more developed imaginative sense; devoid of imagination, it was simply tedious.

I soon had a sentiment of that, and I did not feel any emotion in consequence. Without rage and without despair, my decision was made: I would not write any more. For three months I lived on my chaise longue or standing by the window, to the panes of which I stuck my forehead for hours on end, while my fingers tapped out monotonous music still-born in my mind.

Insensible, I watched life passing by.

A reaction arrived.

I wanted to live the life of Society and of partying. For five years I was a slave of pleasure, or what is called Pleasure, one of the convicts in the prison that is known as High Society, one of the suits that flutter around music halls, theaters and their wings, one of the marionettes who sup at the same table every evening, with the same entourage of gaudily-clad demoiselles playing at drunkenness and seeming to be electrified by Boldi's orchestra while they calculate within themselves, very carefully, the possible sums they can demand from the gentlemen who see them home.

Mistresses! I had enough of them; I wallowed sufficiently in alcoves, from those of the Rue de Prony to the small houses of the queens of the fête, all the way to the furnished apartments of the debutantes of the Rue de La Bruyère; I ran around all the hospitable houses sufficiently, and even woke up often enough in beds ornamented with authentic blazons. And everywhere, I only found Mademoiselle Omnibus, at a full-, half- or a fifth-tariff. I never knew a disinterested kiss, and I never collected the little blue flower that the grisette allows to be taken by her tradesman lover, in the sweet hour of mutual romance. Socialites perhaps had a more delicate fashion of "operating a Monsieur" than prostitutes, but that was the only difference.

In truth, yes, all demoiselles Omnibus. What am I saying? Not even that, for I never found one entirely passive. All of them had a revolt in their eyes and their lips, a dull hatred of slaves for the master, of the dominated for the dominator, in their banal, worn-out, threadbare amorous phrases. That translated into mocking argot on the part of the whore and bilious sarcasm in the woman of the world. Perhaps those women all sensed my indifference, an indifference that wanted to be transformed into passion but could not arrive there; perhaps they read within me my impotence to love, and were afraid of all the indifference that was floating in my eyes at the moment of orgasm.

How derisory were my mistresses! With the exception of the professionals, petty actresses, skaters or simply suppers whose hours are quoted at twenty-five louis to the louis of the traveler, the professionals who, at least don't try to create the belief that they are selling amour, or even the illusion of it, who were they? What were they? Misses Perce-Neige.

One Miss Perce-Neige, a vaguely pretty Scotswoman, eccentrically casual, had a manner of getting to the bottom of things and calling them by their name that did not lack flavor . . . She posed as an amorous and sensual woman, talked to me about the sacrifice of her position and her future and routinely borrowed five hundred louis a month from me under the pretext that the baronet, her father, was late in sending her allowance. One idle afternoon, when I had gone to see whether there was anything interesting going on at Anatole's, the hairdresser in the Cité d'Antin, we came face to face unexpectedly. Miss blushed and mumbled. I left, smiling.

How many misses constructed on the same pattern there were in my existence! And how many Madame Aguerreaus: Angèle Aguerreau, fake blonde and falsely sentimental, who sported a grim husband as a screen, a husband who only talked about honor, fidelity and vengeance, the personification of the "Kill her!" of Dumas fils; he tapped me three times a week in order to regulate, he claimed, his gambling debts, but in reality to keep the marital saucepan on the boil.

And more comtesses of the genre of the vaporous Pole who emerged from a female gypsy orchestra from which her husband had fished her in Vienna one night of partying, in order to make her a grand dame. That one had figured in society but only for one season; one evening she had arrived at a ball almost naked; it appears that Neronian balls were already wearing her out. She had such a success with the messieurs that she was thrown out. From then on, the comte having become useless, she got rid of him. Poor comte! He was ardent, although already past fifty, while the comtesse was . . . knowledgeable. In six months he was cleaned out, shaved and burned, relegated to one of his châteaux in Krakovia with two servants who dressed him, put him to bed and fed him. The comtesse stayed in Paris, in the best house on the Île Saint-Louis, reduced to an annual income of fifty thousand francs—a pittance for her—only seeing men, and a great many of them. Her specialty consisted of getting her hooks into fatigued young men, having them make wills in her favor, burying them, and passing on to the next. Oh, the Comtesse de Slatiwiska! She only saw me three times. I had sniffed the ogress, the succubus.

Oh, my life during those five years! In the end, sickened by all those banalities, I no longer haunted anything but fairgrounds, the facile society of stalls and tents, cynical and extortionate, but in which I could, at least, still find passion.

To those fairgrounds, the nocturnal life of the ill-fated faubourgs, I owe days of unnamable joys and sorrows that were further joys, because it is better to suffer than not to feel. They educated my soul, as a curiosity-seeker and vagabond of vice, a seeker of the absolute who ran around for months, anxiously, appealing for a new sensation of the skin or the soul, going toward impressions of terror, joy or surprise, impressions that were already imprecise as soon as they were sensed.

Curiosity-seeker? Oh, yes. And how many evenings I wasted in those fairgrounds, in wrestling arenas, menageries and even freak shows, the wretched tents of phenomena where mugs are invited for two sous to feel the thighs of a young woman of nineteen who weighs two hundred kilos . . . How many evenings I spent wandering for hours along sinister exterior boulevards, from La Chapelle to the Boulevard d'Italie, on the desolate fortifs, on the perfidious borders from Billancourt-aux-Matelottes to Sanit-Ouen-les-Chiffons, from Pantin-le-Rouge to Saint-Denis-les-Usines, through every suburb that sings and weeps the poverty and prostitution of Paris!

Curiosity-seeker? Oh yes . . . curious for a robustness, a color or a music, a virtue or a vice, a beauty or a flaw—curious, in brief, for an active life that I sensed there, a passionate life that rolled around me, and in which, in spite of all my desires and all my efforts, I could not take part!

Chagrined, I developed a fine passion for traveling, a dangerous element to introduce into existence, and for which I had been only too well prepared by the peregrinations of my father from one garrison to another, the errant life of all families of officers. In two years I scarcely spent two consecutive weeks in Paris, yesterday in Bretagne, tomorrow in Italy, the day after in Oran, all skies and all locations, the ferocious ocher and cobalt of Algeria or the fondant mildness of Venice after the bitter sadness of Armorica . . . voyages use up and blunt sensibility too rapidly. At length, the changing scenery of skies, climates and cities pass before indifferent eyes like a simple panorama. I was like a diver searching the ocean bed for a marvelous pearl, forever undiscoverable, like a squirrel in its cage, turning its wheel endlessly without ever being able to get out; the sensations no longer flourished.

> *Everything is dead! I have traversed worlds,*
> *And I have lost my flight in their milky ways . . .* [1]

---

1 The lines are from "Le Christ aux oliviers" by Gérard de Nerval, from *Les Chimères* (1854).

I returned to Paris, to the Hôtel Mordann. I buried myself in my room, indifferent to the increasingly pronounced hostility of my family, and for three months my life was a Sahara, from which a bird sometimes rose up, fleeing in haste: a vibrant thought of my lassitude, traversing my weary heart.

Then, once again, I woke up—and what an awakening!

I had a need, almost a hunger, for intellectual movement. Irresistibly, my mind rejected all idleness. I wanted to do something: no matter what, but something. I became smitten with reading. I read avidly, without choosing, an intellectual glutton, everything that I found: romances, vaudevilles, memoirs, feuilletons, tragedies, histories, tales of literary cobblers: Baudelaire, Ramollot,[1] Mendès, Richebourg, Verlaine, Villiers de l'Isle Adam, Ohnet, Rachilde, Flaubert, Laforgue, Louis Noir, d'Aurevilly, Sarcey, Lorrain, Anatole France, Jules Mary, Tailhade, Essebac,[2] Jean Lombard, Méténier, Zola . . . what do I know?

---

[1] Colonel Ramollot was the hero of a series of action-adventure novels by the prolific Charles Leroy (1844-1895). Andhré's reading list alternates highbrow and lowbrow writers with a deliberate incongruity; Émile Richebourg (1833-1898) was a prolific and very popular feuilletoniste, and the journalist Louis Noir (1837-1901) became a prolific writer of action-adventure novels set in far-flung locations: a career trajectory subsequently followed by Fabrice, probably under the influence of his reading of Noir, Richebourg and Leroy

[2] "Achille Essebac" (Achille Bécasse, 1868-1936) had recently published *Dédé* (1901), a scandalous homoerotic novel; he was an associate of Jacques Adelswärd-Fersen, whose exile from Paris in 1903 following lurid newspaper "exposés" of his fondness for staging "living tableaux" has been previously noted. Essebac issued some work via the original publisher of *L'Araignée rouge*.

That indigestion of literature, laminated with loaves of bread, cutlets and strawberries in ether,[1] sauerkraut and beef cooked in honey, unhinged me temporarily for some months, when I went astray, equally unselectively in foreign literatures—Spanish, English, Italian and Polish. When I had completed all the vagaries of people who read several languages, my reflections became entangled in bizarre ways. I formulated metaphysical speculations in the language of feuilletons; simple ideas were enunciated bristling with unusual terms. I blurred everything. The pleasantries of Allais were magnified by the beautiful style of Loti.

I suffered so much from all of that that I stopped reading abruptly, and my mind gradually recovered its former torpor . . . but alas, I returned to it, this time, and permanently. Dolorous . . . My quiet lassitude was over! I knew idleness populated with vague and profound apprehensions, a bitterness overlay my idle life. I lived through innumerable painful meditations, time wasted, irremediably, sunk in the past—blond crops dead underfoot, grapes dried up without vintages . . .

Spleen, terrible spleen, bit my heart.

Annihilated by my impotence, I was devoid of the courage to construct an illusion of work. I did not even have the will power necessary to employ myself in some useful and banal labor, the realization of which would not leave any room within me for anxiety. For days and

---

1 Strawberries steeped in ether was a gourmet treat notoriously publicized by Jean Lorrain, in collaboration with Liane de Pougy, in whose home it was allegedly consumed in the mid-1890s.

nights I was slumped in the monotony of an existence adrift, which a sharp anguish tortured with crises.

It was then that I made the acquaintance of my friend, my confidant, my consoler, the one that is always there: ether.

One day, when I was suffering atrociously from gastric neuralgia, Doctor de Fauvières prescribed a few drops of ether. My physical illness disappeared; and my intellectual person, so weak and debilitated, felt vivified, as if born to a new existence. I then had, and very clearly, the sentiment that I was alive, that my being, previously in limbo, was awakening to joy, in the light, in paradise: a white, cold paradise.

I became better for others, more amenable for myself. Something generous and strong exalted my person, changed my weakness into firmness. It really was all joy, all paradise and all of paradise that was within me.

And for months I lived that dream of perfect happiness. I stood up to life and its troubles. I was the master, the king, the god of my universe. I had the entire sentiment that no power, no cataclysm, could rob me of the joy of my existence or poison it by means of the memory—the bitter memory—of my defunct sorrows.

Ether! Ether! What sweet hours do I not owe to you! Your kiss of light froze and dissipated my anguish, abolished my old torture. Thanks to you, I have strength and quietude. My vagabond imagination understands your agreeable chimeras. You nuance my thoughts from black to white, passing through all the golds, blues and crimsons. All light dissolves into particles in my soul and I evolve, I am refined, I am purified in an ascension toward the Beautiful.

And I resumed my reading, slowly, one by one. A great deal wearied me. Gradually, I no longer read anything but purely imaginative works or those that offered new, unforeseen perceptions, discoveries of bizarre, odd sensations. Tales of a coldly extravagant, often ferocious, humor charmed me, but fatigued me rapidly. Once more, the literature of hallucination and fantasy failed me. Only the tableau of broad visions, rapid and truly adventurous adventures still seduced and excited me. They pleased me above all, those adventures, because they offered me the possibility of increasing them, of magnifying them in my reveries, of almost living them by substituting my soul, in thought, for that of the author.

A bizarre thing! Very often, thus, I continued books whose subjects stopped too short, simplified and quickly resolved, too quickly for my liking. To the second Faust I added a third Faust. I created new tortures for Mickiewicz's Konrad Wallenrod.[1] I made Don Juan travel to other lands and dry up his tears in feasting. I tormented for weeks the last night of Gérard de Nerval before enabling him to hang himself in the Rue de la Vieille-Lanterne—Gérard de Nerval, the only poet I love, and whose verses rise to

---

1 *Konrad Wallenrod* (1826) is a narrative poem by the Polish writer Adam Mickiewicz set in fourteenth-century Lithuania, a thinly-disguised protest against the partition of eighteenth-century Poland and Lithuania by Russia, Prussia and the Hapsburg monarchy. The poem helped to inspire an uprising in 1830 against Russian rule. The pagan Konrad is Christianized and joins the Order of Teutonic Knights, but is recalled to his heritage by an enigmatic minstrel, and commits "patriotic treason" before killing himself: a controversial exemplar.

my lips continually, like prayers. All those puerile reveries I enjoyed and suffered delectably.

And then, suddenly, that quietude and that joy capsized, like theatrical scenery disappearing before the spectator's eyes. My older sister followed her husband—an officer, obviously—to the Midi. My father died abruptly a fortnight after that departure, and my mother, frightened by her solitude, brought into her presence, in order to keep her company, the classic poor relative, my cousin Louisette.

The departure of my sister and the death of my father left my eyes dry. I was too indifferent to them for them not to be indifferent to me. Is it my fault if my family had done nothing to conquer the love of the child?

There was only one change for me. My dear cousin Louisette, with the exquisite sensibility of individuals who have suffered from poverty, came to cheer up my solitude, in the high room where I had cloistered myself with a view of the deserted boulevards of the Barrière d'Italie, the chalky mass of the Butte-aux-Cailles, the multicolored Bièvre, the gardens of the Gobelins and, when my windows were open, the odors of that landscape of leprosies and roses: tanned skins, the verdure of the Gobelins and the indefinable reek of Algerian solitude that, from spring until autumn, the eccentric quarter where our family house offers all the equivocal quality of a dwelling of the Marquis de Sade.

Louisette? She is a Sister of Charity. It is now for six months that she has been attentive to my moods, sometimes forcing me to laugh, to break the hostility of my silence, "civilizing" me, says Maman, who already sees her as my future wife. She has brought me closer to my mother, and has restored to me a little interest in living. Who knows? Perhaps her soul has confused the sentiment of my anguish and my terrors?

"Andhré! Are you coming down to dinner?"

It's her who has come into my room like a gust of wind, an entire springtime in her eyes and in the creases of her dress, an entire springtime in her figure and her slightly unkempt hair, her blonde hair, the blonde of liquid gold. And she obliges me to abandon my chaise longue, drags me away, makes me run downstairs, and I, although so sad today, arrive before a mother in mourning, in the dining room sparkling in its crystal and its sprightly Morlais porcelain, her eyes luminous and her mouth laughing.

II

THE August of roses has passed and perished, monotonously...

How I hate the country, all that verdure that at first reposed, and then exasperated me, the ignoble country, dirty and greasy, the dung-heaps drying out and becoming noxious, the fruit trees devoid of beauty but which "produce." Are my soul and my senses of a city-dweller made to live in this immutable décor of excessively verdant hills, forests, where one cannot muse, trailing an umbrella, without the risk of breaking one's neck at every step? And those ugly village houses, earthen, and their thatch, which is more dung—the dung under which the peasants live; all those houses, cowsheds! And those graceless church bells... And the rustics who salute me, sniggering, with a mocking expression, hostile eyes—is it me that anyone is going to tell that they are my fellows? How many idle generations would it require to change the form of their hands, to render them gracious and fit company for good-looking people?

The hands! I have always been haunted by beautiful hands, slightly plump, sinewy, the fingers tapering and the almond-shaped nails pink . . . agile hands, caressant hands . . . above all, hands that "embrace." For me, all sensibility is found in the hands. There are virtuous hands, sanguine hands, with a strong embrace, and culpable hands, hands that abandon themselves and whose embrace is soft . . . it is only in cities that I have found those hands.

"You don't like the country, then?" Maman often asks me. "You don't experience any pleasure in the country?"

"The pleasures of the country, Maman, are a bad invention of feuilletonistes short of copy. No, I'm not idyllic. Personally, the country doesn't make me vomit verses. I don't wax ecstatic about the beauty of panoramas, the fresh faces of peasant women. I don't amuse myself picking violets, pansies and hyacinths in the woods. I don't have the soul of a milliner so dear to contemporary poets. When I desire a bouquet I telegraph Paris and I receive the flowers the next day. I detest clumsy peasant bouquets composed with no regard for form and the arrangement of colors. And as for 'good milk, pure air and fresh eggs'—a bad joke!"

Oh, the exhausting walks along long rectilinear roads, with their poplars, making phantasmal reverences in the wind, their houses dozing in the vespertine heaviness, when the atmosphere shines soundlessly under the expansion of an oriental sun and the wind passes in brief waves over the silent valley . . .

"It's exercise that he needs," Doctor de Fauvières has declared—I know that thanks to Louisette's confidence. "That big lad has been sequestered, voluntarily. Pure air and long walks will calm his nerves."

Maman is making me follow the doctor's prescriptions to the letter, without suspecting that my mental state is too afflicted for walks to be able to cure my incurable melancholy. And then, my walks are so solitary, in spite of the continual presence of Louisette, her gaiety and her babble . . . A few minutes after our departure from the house, she is infected by my mutism; her pleasantries and her laughter congeal, so to speak, on her lips, and silence—a frightful silence that neither of us has the courage to break—weighs upon us until we return. When we arrive at the gate of the château, like schoolchildren afraid of being caught at fault, we exchange futile remarks, and Maman doesn't divine all the tears there are beneath my feigned cheerfulness.

Tears for what, shed over what? I don't know. They're tears over the impossibility of my having a goal in existence, a truly elevated goal, a conquest, which is worth the trouble of battling or striving. I am too well aware of my impotence to create a work, and that is why something has gone awry within me: the interest of living.

To whom can I confide my pain? To whom can I recount my anguish? To Louisette? In spite of all her efforts, she doesn't understand; she would lavish me with consolations that would exasperate me. For instance, she would tell me that it's necessary to try to write, that perhaps I would arrive, by dint of perseverance, at finding a way, etc. etc. . . . an irritating viaticum that would make me detest the poor girl. My mother? She would smile indulgently, and, under the pretext of calming me down, would chide the "big lad" for having no energy, or even remind me severely that I didn't want to follow the path traced by my father. Ask for counsel from religion? All the cults, with their monstrous pharisaism, are odious to me—and occultism, that religion of yesterday and tomorrow, frightens me. So?

So, I'm increasingly convinced that

> *Like a name engraved in tree-bark*
> *A memory hollows out progressively.*[1]

And of the despairing thought of Heinrich Heine: "We live in intellectual solitude." Yes, we are all solitary. No thought penetrates another thought deeply enough for there to be a communion of souls. We all live in intellectual solitude.

Other men, however, frequent other men; a society exists, amuses itself and narcotizes itself. How vain its pleasures seem to me! People scarcely take pleasure except in the company of their fellows. And I feel very alone.

---

1 Gérard de Nerval, from "La Grand-mère," in *Odelettes* (1853).

III

A displacement has interested me: a week-long sojourn in Noyon, to which, with Maman's consent, I have emigrated. I was stifling in Carlepont.

My hotel room overlooks a rather vast square, the paving stones of which disappear completely under weeds and moss. Pigeons frolic and coo all day long without being disturbed in the slightest. In the middle of the square there is a Gothic fountain, very slender, delicately perforated like lace, clad in curious yellow-tinted gray fungus, singing over a green bowl. All the gables of the houses are turned toward the square and gaze lugubriously at the fountain and its circling avian frolics. By day one might think those dwellings uninhabited, but in the evening all the little windows with blank panes light up, remaining illuminated long before dark. It is a strange vision, that of the houses, which seem to be celebrating in the darkness the cult of Amphitrite around a noisy jet of water.

Noyon! I find there, in each of my sojourns, a little calm and interest in living. I love its tortuous little poorly-paved streets, its leaning houses, its ogival windows and doors, its cathedral, extending its desperate arms toward the sky, and its fan-like Place des Chanoines.

Some streets, in particular, have an indescribable charm, and I delight in spending hours there. Silence reigns there all day long, a heavy silence that hangs and lulls. They are true back-streets of very old towns, provincial corners still preserving the habits of the curfew, where the passage of an auto seems a frightful anachronism. Behind crumbling walls, here and there, are immense gardens, all gray, where majestically aligned trees recall the great century.

In one of the more improbably "provincial" streets, twice a day—at midday, when the sun attaches golden and vermilion threads to the bronze and rusty iron of high and narrow casements, and at six o'clock in the evening, when the agony of the sun still slashes the windows with gold and blood—little girls clad in pale blue with red belts play, stamping their feet on the stones, which render a sound like that of the tide on shingle. Now, at the end of August, there are a dozen at the most playing in the garden, a dozen schoolgirls who have not departed on vacation, and they alone trouble the reign of the silence that is established in old Noyon, where the calm, calm life is absorbed by the sky; old Noyon, in which the hours fall, roll and die like a knell.

Other back-streets also solicit and attract my black soul, miry back-streets when countless clothes hang out of the windows, and the gables tend to join their counterparts, where spiders have suspended their webs between the roofs, weaving triumphal arches in the gloom and porticoes of forgetfulness. Yes, I love them, those streets; I love to disturb the stones placed at an angle against the walls, in order to gaze at the swarming insects, and then crush them underfoot.

Insects! They had always been a source of fear and joy since childhood—a delightful fear, which gives me the frisson of the *petit mort* every time. That is inexplicable. I loved to watch those unknown brightly-colored and strangely-formed creatures flying through the air. I loved their opaline wings, their hairy corselets. And suddenly, abruptly, a cruelty came to me. I ripped off their wings and then watched them dragging themselves on the ground, in the dust and the mud, running on their legs, so delicate and so flexible, suffering, doubtless terribly. Then I ripped off their legs, all except one. I tipped them over and contemplated that leg, agitating desperately, that poor leg, which enabled me to observe life in the insect. I spent frightful and joyful minutes saturating my eyes with that agony.

In recent days, fortuitously, doubtless because I saw the little schoolgirls walking in their large garden, holding cages full of flies, my infantile soul rose again within me and resumed its place. And I, who faint at a bullfight, protest against the brutality of carters and have a horror of suffering, grotesquely, I spend entire afternoons in the dark stinking back-streets displacing stones in order to have the pleasure of squashing insects.

That is where idleness has led me, at the age of thirty. I'm pitiful. I'm going back to Carlepont. In the company of my mother and Louisette, these follies will pass, I'm sure.

IV

I have been back in Carlepont for ten days, but the obsession has not quit me. The infantile soul that I thought dead, which has been resuscitated so fortuitously, appears to want to install itself despotically. It is taking me away, distantly; I don't know where. I sense, however, that the world in which I am going to live is nothing but darkness and sobs.

I have been conquered by a bestial pleasure: I trap flies, in order to intoxicate myself with hideous and ridiculous spectacles, in order to throw them, alive, into spider-webs. That amusement renders me more solitary, for I hide it from Maman and Louisette. If they discovered my joys, how they would laugh at me! Ironically, for sure, Maman would buy me a dozen fly-cages.

The fear of ridicule prevented me, during the first twenty-four hours after my return from Noyon, from delivering myself to my renascent passion. Scarcely was I reinstalled in my room, however, resuming the life of the château, than the torturing thought became imperious; and I yielded to it.

The important thing was to go out alone, without Louisette. I achieved that by simulating a need for activity. I pretended to desire ardently to travel the roads, to intoxicate myself with air and liberty.

"Hurrah for the bicycle!" I said to Maman. "Hurrah for exercise!"

She applauded that whim, which, for her and for Louisette, constitutes a forward step toward a cure.

So I go out alone, affecting a cheerful and determined attitude. I launch myself through the village at top speed, to the great amazement of the inhabitants. They have known me so bleak and desolate until now! And when I have gone around the park, when I'm sure that no inquisitive gaze is attached to me, I park the bicycle in a ditch and lie down in the mossy grass, the wilting grass of September, and I observe the spiders.

In all directions I perceive their webs, extended in concentric circles, displayed in carpets, suspended in curtains and elongated garlands. The plants, the trees—bark and branches—the soil, the furrows, the stones and all the natural bodies placed in the open air, under the vault of the sky, are covered by their threads: threads of an extreme tenuity, invisible in darkness but whose brightness enables them to be seen in sunlight; threads that design fragile masterpieces.

Watchful, in a corner of their web, the spiders wait . . . and when I throw the fly, the long legs agitate, rise and fall, twist, dance and lap. Oh, the feverish legs that are activated by precipitate movements! And the eyes, microscopic drops of sardonyx, which roll ferociously in the black heads, the eyes that give the impression of watching the feet, the long, hooked legs that are always "knitting," until the moment when the prey, stunned, remains inert, when the mouth approaches, the hairy little tongue drooling over the quivering palps.

I can distinguish them all now, from the garden spiders with emerald and gold robes and formidable jaws to the tarantulas with gray-green corselets striped with gold, and the gray harvest spiders with thin and immeasurably long legs, which make them resemble animals mounted on articulated and mobile stilts, and the hideous black funnel-web spiders with short hairy legs, bodies like hazelnuts and eight carbuncle eyes. However, spiders frighten me. At the mere thought that one might let itself go to the end of its thread and touch my skin, run over my face or over my arm, I get up and run away, instantly nauseated; I feel a vertigo, as if I were going mad. I run straight ahead, jumping over ditches, tracing a path through the undergrowth. Sometimes, in my crazy course, I run straight into invisible spider-webs. Then, dazed, I make convulsive gestures to rub my face and hands; a shudder shakes my whole body and I utter cries of fright . . .

Then, of my own accord, I calm down; I laugh at my terror and my disgust, and I capture a few more flies, which I throw once again as prey to the spiders.

V

I am fleeing Carlepont and the Noyonnais; I could no longer live there.

These last days I spent in the most remote part of the park, near an old stone bench clad in a flowery blanket of lichens and mosses, at the extremity of a broad avenue of centenarian oaks, the foliage of which forms a somber vault as cool as a nave. There, I had discovered a colony of funnel-web spiders, and, in order to see them emerge from their retreats, I remained lying for hours, my entire being resolute in one obsession: the black spiders. At the bloody hour of sunset they showed themselves, agitating all their feet like the tentacles of a squid, and it was then that I presented them with flies, which they came to seize almost from my fingertips.

Who can imagine my horror at the thought that they might touch me!

Two evenings ago, Louisette, who was wandering in the park, perceived me accomplishing the suspect task of feeding spiders. I didn't see her; but later, during dinner, she joked amiably, before Maman:

"Andhré is becoming very kind."

"What do you mean, little cousin?"

"You know very well. Come on, don't play the innocent. I saw you, and I know everything. I saw you just now in the park. You were doubtless giving breadcrumbs to a little bird, for you were approaching very gently, gently . . . I kept my distance, in order not to embarrass you.

"Good," said Maman, smiling. "You're becoming a bird-charmer."

How that Louisette frightened me! If she had really seen . . . what if she knew . . . !

So, tomorrow, unable to stay any longer in Carlepont, having given the pretext of buying an automobile, I shall buckle my trunks and valises and leave for Paris.

Who can tell? Perhaps this flight is my salvation, the cure of the mania that, I sense, has taken over me completely. In Paris, the infantile soul that has reawakened within me will go to sleep again; I shall be rid of that obsession, and, at the same time, of all my incurable melancholy.

Oh, to be able to look at and smell a rose, to repose my eyes on a fresh face! Oh, to be able to hear, love and hate, to flee analysis, the torturing analysis that pursues me even into my nocturnal dreams! Like old Faust, I want to make spring forth from the depths of my desiccated heart the crazy fount of life, beautiful, ardent and excessive . . .

VI

I knew that in Paris the nascent obsession would vanish, but what I did not suspect is that hope would enter my heart again at the same time. And yet it has. Since yesterday, I have hope.

An appearance at the Hôtel Mordann, the time to deposit my trunks, and I departed into life, at random, without any other goal than forgetting, forgetting my childhood, that childhood kneaded by cruelty, which had loomed up before me for several weeks, melted gradually into my soul, and was beginning to take possession of my will. I spent the whole afternoon looking in the numerous bookshops on the quay and in the cool streets of the Monnaie quarter, for dusty and saffroned books ornamented with armories, whose bindings had a history, a history in which I had interested myself for years.

At dusk, an unlucky hunter, I was following the Quai des Grands-Augustins pensively, interrogating myself regarding the possible goal of my evening. Dinner at home, at the club or in the Champs-Élysées scarcely appealed to me. I was truly at a loss. Before my eyes were the houses of the Île de la Cité, narrow, high and crowded, like a band of old pauper women gathered in a flock, houses splashed with the magic of the sunset, gleams of copper and green gold; on the Seine, calm and shiny, as if silvered, heavy barges were asleep, raising here and there toward the mauve sky the futile crosses of their masts and yard-arms: a scene escaped from the palette of a Flemish master or Lebourg,[1] the painter of the Parisian banks.

I was sketching projects for the evening as best I could: dinner in the Champs-Élysées or an iced drink at some spectacle of women—that was what I was reduced to!—and even commencing to put them into execution when someone tapped me familiarly on the shoulder. I turned round and recognized Comte Pierre de Nidine, a friend of college and partying—especially partying—of whom I had lost sight three or four years earlier

"Aha!" he said, laughing. "Are you meditating a volume of verses for the solitary stroller in these misty solitudes, or have you fallen in love?"

"Neither."

"It's serious, then."

He linked arms with me in a familiar fashion.

"To quit you four years ago in the middle of Mustapha-Supérieur, while wandering one evening with Carmenvita and that Lili Sombreuse, who was fonder of you than you were of her, one evening—or rather one night—in which we'd done a little too much wandering around the Moorish cafés of low Algeria, and then to find you again, just as detached from human things, at least in appearance, in the heart of modern Paris, a few paces

---

[1] Albert Lebourg (1849-1928), an impressionist landscape painter fond of working on the banks of the Seine in the suburbs of Paris.

from the noisy student boulevard, is piquant, you must admit! I ought to leave you to get bored on your own at twenty louis an hour, but I don't have the heart . . . and then, this evening, my dear Andhré, I'm a bachelor. You'll dine with me!"

And in spite of my resistance, that great fool Nidine, one of the rare companions with whom I had ever sympathized in my life, dragged me away and shoved me into a carriage. Half an hour later, in a boulevard restaurant, we ordered a meal. And while the waiters hastened around, Pierre chatted, joyfully, veritably joyful to see me again and to tell me about his life during the last four years, the fashion in which he had broken with the riotous life, racecourses and chatterers and (I was going to laugh) had married! Really? Honestly? Yes, he was married. He had had enough, in the end, of the life devoid of dignity and honor, in which his name, the name of the Nidines, one of the ancient families of France, counting maréchals and cardinals, illustrious writers, and even a saint, which had illuminated the entire eighteenth century after having aided the Bourbons to sit on the throne—a Nidine had died for the Béarnais—had fallen as far as the owner of a racing stable, to serve as a sign for shady bookmakers and other horse enthusiasts. Yes, he had married, scarcely six months ago, and married to his taste, without any prejudice of caste, the daughter of a great sculptor, Claude Dereyer . . . and now he was happy, truly happy. He only lived for his wife, and his wife adored him.

All of that confession was made with the enthusiastic tone of an infatuated man. He was not mistaken, and did not deceive me. His eyes, once dead, now brilliant, and his voice, once ironic, now convincing and assured, indicated a Nidine who was master of his happiness. His happiness? He exalted it to me, painting it with passionate words throughout dinner, without even giving me the possibility of getting a word in—which I scarcely thought of doing.

That good Nidine, what a tender and amorous heart he had hidden for so long beneath his feigned skepticism! At dessert, with his elbows on the table and looking me in the eyes, drunk on speech and mineral water, he admitted his disenchantment with partying. He too had been one of those who suffered in silence, dissimulating their tears behind a mask of gaiety. But now that he had escaped from that Hell, now that he had conquered happiness—that word always returned to his lips—he admitted his secret tortures of old, the ever-compressed leaps of his imagination, his thirst for amour, which he had never been able to appease on any mouth.

How he warmed me up with his enthusiasm; how much good those cries of a soul in Purgatory finally risen to Paradise did me! How he praised with conviction the joys of his marriage, the life of amour beside the wife one loves and also esteems!

"True happiness," he concluded, continually, "is in the amour, reputedly ridiculous, that one has the good fortune to find; in the bourgeois amour uniting two lovers who love one another in all honesty."

Dear Nidine!

"Well," I said to him, interrupting him for the first time since the commencement of the dinner, "for a man so in love with his wife and his hearth, you seem to be neglecting both this evening. Here you are at the cabaret, dining like a bachelor."

"Pardon me," Nidine replied, hotly, "but I'm no deserter."

And he explained to me that the comtesse had gone to spend a few days in Normandy with her family, and that he had not been able to accompany her. She was returning that evening by a train arriving in Paris at eleven-twenty at the Gare Saint-Lazare. With that, he summoned the waiter and asked for the bill, which I amused myself by settling in spite of his protests.

"Well, so be it; you're at home in the restaurant," he declared, "but I'll have my revenge when you wish to give us the pleasure of dining at the house. In fact," he added, "you have nothing to do, have you? No amorous rendezvous or engagement with friends? Well, come with me to the Gare Saint-Lazare. I'll introduce you to Geneviève."

We left the restaurant and I accompanied him to the station. On the way, between two puffs of cigar-smoke, I was subjected to another edition of happiness in marriage. Nidine, my friend Nidine, repeated himself a little too much. However, it was not disagreeable. It even distracted me momentarily from my melancholia—the melancholia expressed by my silence, which Nidine, as egotistical as all lovers, did not perceive. So prolix regarding his own life, he did not care about mine.

We arrived at the Gare Saint-Lazare at eleven-twenty, the hour shown on the exterior clock; and without worrying about the carriage stationed in the Cour Du Havre, he jumped.

"Oh! Let's go up quickly. We're late . . . she might be waiting."

He launched himself forward, climbing the stairs four at a time, bustled the employee at the gate, and we arrived, out of breath, to learn that the Granville express was eight minutes late.

"What luck!" said Nidine. "You'll excuse me, won't you, for being a little . . . hasty, but . . ."

"The Comtesse de Nidine mustn't be kept waiting," I finished, smiling, while dear Pierre, entirely given to the joy of seeing his lovely wife again, darted watchful eyes into the hall.

The wail of a siren, two yellow gleams in a black form that was eating up the rails, and the train appeared; a hand gloved in white suede at the door of a compartment that opened, and the comte drew into his arms, rather than aiding her to descend, a slim young woman in a very simple traveling costume. Gluttonous kisses under the mocking gazes of passers-by. That was slightly common; I was embarrassed by it, but it was charming. A minute later, remembering me, Pierre murmured, while I bowed:

"My dear Geneviève . . . Monsieur Andhré Mordann, one of my childhood friends, rediscovered a few hours ago after four years of separation. Andhré wanted to accompany me this far in order to present his homages to you."

"Too kind, Monsieur," replied a pearly voice. "Pierre has often mentioned you to me; I would be glad to see you at our home, in order that Pierre and you can, not renew, but consolidate again the bonds of affection that unite you."

I returned the compliment by raising my eyes to Comtesse Geneviève de Nidine. The fresh, rosy face, of a very regular oval, had all the mildness of a pastel. It was illuminated by a bright and luminous gaze. But what astonished and attracted at the same time in that Latour[1] was the frank mouth, of a firm design, with sensual lips. That mouth was maddening. It invited kisses.

We left the station. The couple went to the carriage.

"By the way," asked Nidine, enquiring about me and my life for the first time, "Are you still living with your mother? Would you like us to drop you at her door?"

"No need. It would take you too far out of your way, and Madame de Nidine must be tired."

"That's true," the young woman declared, "I admit frankly that I'm exhausted."

"As you please," said my friend But one of these days . . . as soon as possible . . . 38 Rue de Chateaubriand. *À bientôt*, Andhré."

The carriage drew away with a noise of little bells, and was lost. I stayed there for a minute on the edge of the sidewalk, and then threw myself into a fiacre and had myself taken to the Hôtel Mordann.

All along the way, and even having entered the house and gone to bed, I dreamed about the happiness conquered by Pierre de Nidine; on closing my eyes I saw again the face of the comtesse, her voluptuous mouth, and a kind of voice murmured to me, in a breath, in my ear: "Hope!"

The night was devoid of nightmares. I slept.

---

1 Henri Fantin-Latour (1836-1904), a Romantic painter who was especially fond of depicting faces and flowers.

VII

MIGHT I be in love with Madame de Nidine, by chance—a quasi-providential chance that might save me from my anguish?

For two days, that question has tormented me, and I dare not respond to it. In love, me? That would be truly droll, and I would pay with the luxury of being ridiculous in my own eyes. In love! But that's a very old game, and too new for me, who, since my seventeenth year and even a little before, on the school benches, played the comedy of being blasé, and perhaps really was, by virtue of a vague intuition, for fear of amour. Who can tell?

Might I be in love with Madame de Nidine—Geneviève?

That is my sword of Damocles. And that stabbing pain is almost a joy.

Yes, for two days I run right and left all over Paris, busying myself and enthusing myself for everything and nothing. I wander around the Louvre and intoxicate myself with Watteau, the only painter of the past who was truly French, with the Clouets and Philippe de Champaigne. I go into galleries of modern painting, chez Georges Petit, Durand-Ruel or the Bernheims, in order to intoxicate myself with Renoir, the smiles of his women, their coquetry, their anxious and feline grace: Renoir, the unique painter of the woman of the end of the nineteenth century; Renoir, a talent that is directly united with the eighteenth, the true painter, as Degas is the true draughtsman, of our epoch.

Renoir! It is before his voluptuous figures that I have rediscovered the amorous lips of which I dream, those lips made for sensuality—the very lips of Madame de Nidine. It is thanks to the complicity of that great artist that I savor exquisite minutes.

But my life, for two days, has been a continual fanfare, a re-entry into the world of the living and the beautiful, of robust reality. I am cheerful; I sing; the present and the future smile at me; yesterday evening I quivered at Gustave Charpentier's *Louise*;[1] at midnight I emerged from the Opera-Comique, drunk on music and healthy joys.

Might this be amour? This need to love all humanity and commune with it, this intoxication that impels a smile, at everyone, to find grace in passers-by, the clans of the streets—yes, truly, to smile at all the women because one cherishes one of them, and because in all the feminine faces encountered one believes that one recognizes

---

1 Charpentier's opera *Louise*, premiered in 1900, was a groundbreaking *avant garde* work with a libretto by the composer and the Symbolist poet Saint-Pol-Roux. The story is a proto-surrealist study of Parisian working-class life and love; it became a big hit all over Europe, although Fabrice could not have known that when he wrote this chapter.

something of her; a remembrance of the lips, the dear red lips, glimpsed for a minute—only one—but the vision of which has remained luminous?

The nascent Phantom is asleep. I no longer sense it except in rare moments, like a sound that is fading and dying away, like a wave of apprehension. It is, it must be, going away; it is going to go away, isn't it?

Might I be in love with Madame de Nidine? Oh, amour, amour at any price!

VIII

WELL, no; I'm not in love with her. I had a presentiment of it. I simply have for her and her husband a great fraternal amity. So, those two days of agitation were a fine illusion. My panics, my flights elsewhere, my profound despairs and my foolish hopes—futile! And the shameful projects of adultery that rose up in my feverish head were sketched at a pure loss. The nascent amour is dead, scarcely born. Yes,

> . . . *suddenly, it melted.*
> *Like a glacier suspended*
> *Over an abyss*

as the dolorous lover of George Sand wrote.[1]

I count now in my life a fraternity in two volumes, Pierre and Geneviève. And that's all, But that "and that's all" is infinitely precious to me

My misfortune—but is it truly a misfortune?—was revealed to me this evening. I was dining in their small

---

1 Alfred de Musset, in "À mon frère, revenant d'Italie" (1844), nowadays best know for its adaptation as a song by Georges Brassens.

house in the Rue de Chateaubriand, a trifle nondescript, a trifle Third Empire *gâteau*, in which the furniture, the paintings and the *objets d'art* have been assembled at random, in accordance with the ridiculous fashion that makes modern apartments resemble a second-hand furniture store, authentic Louis XV next to the hideous modern style.

At the end of my first visit, at the moment when I was about to retire, Pierre retained me in order to share their supper. At table, I found myself placed between the comtesse and him, the comtesse in a becoming lawn costume, reminiscent of a pink rose in a bowl of milk; and after having run the gamut of the usual mundanities, news items in the *Figaro* and the *Gaulois*, announcements of engagements, deaths and receptions, projects for soirées in the coming winter, important premières on the horizon in theaters and sacristies, Nidine, in order not to lose the habit of it, commenced to tell the rosary of conjugal joys under the enamored eyes of his young wife. For I could not be mistaken about it; she had enamored eyes and her lips were drinking in every one of the phrases uttered by her husband. If Pierre adored Geneviève, Geneviève reciprocated. I clearly had that impression and, at the same time, that of the inanity, the ridiculousness, of my amorous disturbance. The scales fell from my eyes. Come on, did I not have to be stupid to believe in the possibility of a redemption? What folly was mine!

Like an awakened bat chased away by bright sunlight, going to batter its head against every wall, my head vacillated, so to speak. For a minute, I was terribly unhappy. The glimpsed paradise closed. I fell from the height of my hope.

Suddenly, the smiling comtesse interrogated me: "And you, Monsieur Mordann, are you going to continue living Pierre's old life?—pardon my question—or have you had enough? Are you weary of the continual carnival?"

And her bright eyes fixed on mine.

"Oh," said Pierre, without giving me time to respond, "Andhré is very different from me. He's never partied excessively, to tell the truth. He's always kept in the margins, Can you imagine, my dear Geneviève, that as I've already told you twenty times, that this big fellow has played, and is doubtless still playing, the exile from enjoyment, the disinherited and the tenebrous beau:

He is the tenebrous, the widowed, the unconsoled
Prince of Aquitaine of the abolished tower;
His only star is dead and his constellated lute
Bears the black sun of melancholy."[1]

Then, continuing in a tone of amicable mockery: "Andhré, my dear Andhré, you play Gérard de Nerval, on the border of the nineteenth century and without the excuse of a Jenny Colon."[2]

---

1 The first lines of Gérard de Nerval's famous sonnet "El Dedischado" (1853), transposed from the first person into the third. The poem was notoriously composed in a lunatic asylum, where Nerval was recovering from a delusional episode, and likens its narrator to a hero abducted, as in the oft-recycled thirteenth-century romance of Ogier le Danois [Ogier the Dane], by an equivocal fay. The poem was later to be quoted by T. S. Eliot in "The Waste Land," a classic exemplar of the same splenetic state of mind.

2 Jenny Colon (1808-1842) was an actress and singer; Gérard de Nerval and Alexandre Dumas provided the libretto for Hippolyte Monpou's *Piquillo* (1836), in which she performed, after which Nerval allegedly became infatuated with her, and was devastated when

And, without reflection, he related a few of my old follies, my singular caprices for rings, cats and parrots, mixing up everything to make a Russian salad of baroque fantasies that had rendered me somewhat legendary in the demi-monde of literature, the arts and the theater. In truth, yes, it had all happened, hidden in rather shady places, even my singular passion for candles. I was embarrassed, and doubtless so visibly embarrassed that the comtesse interrupted her husband.

"In truth, Monsieur Mordann, what joys could you find in spoiling your health and your existence thus?"

And the bright eyes attached themselves to me, interrogatively—so sympathetically interrogative that a great sob rose in my breast and, in a flood, I cried my secret tortures, the malady of doubt that was within me, that malady of excessive sensation, thus and always, that was attached to my soul like a rust, buzzing in my ears like a swarm of obstinate wasps . . . Oh, my agonizing struggles, my need to breathe, to live life like everyone else, to love and to hate!

Did I clamor them sufficiently? Did I say enough about my suffering, my soul struggling in the mesh of the spider-web, incessantly broken and incessantly re-tightened, woven by the indefatigable idea, like a fog over my mind? Oh, yes, I explained my pain sufficiently, the

---

she married a flautist in 1838. She is widely thought to have been the remote inspiration for the hallucinatory novella "Aurélie ou le Rêve et la Vie" (1855), written immediately before the poet's suicide, an obvious precursor of Fabrice's novel. Whether or not Fabrice had "the excuse of a Jenny Colon" is unknown, although the most plausible candidates for the role, if one assumes that he was attracted to women, are Liane de Pougy and Polaire (alias Lili Mamour).

entanglement of my entire being in the search for the absolute of sensation, my descent toward the immutable foundations of sensuality, the certain catastrophe that was awaiting me on the day when my brain, seized by vertigo, would oscillate like the deck of a boat on the liquid back of I know not what chimerical ocean . . .

"Poor Andhré!" Pierre responded to me. "And I was a hundred leagues from suspecting your mental distress! Excuse me . . . ! Listen—would you like us to be your physicians . . . ? Yes . . . ? Come to see us often. By means of contact with us, I'm sure that you can be cured. Above all, it's necessary to live with life, without reasoning, without jibbing . . . letting yourself be captured by it . . . Don't seek happiness, wait for it to arrive, from no matter where, in no matter what milieu, at no matter what moment . . . and when it's within your reach, it's necessary to seize it with a firm hand and not to let it escape, for it only brushes us once . . . But above all, live . . . live!"

And on those consoling words, I quit the young household. Pierre's hands were shaking; the sapphires of the comtesse's eyes were more luminous than ever; they now seemed to be two beacons illuminated by a fraternal hope . . .

Without the candor of those gazes fixed upon me during my confession, I might perhaps have confessed everything—yes, everything, including my secret torture of spiders, that puerile, ridiculous torture, which maddened me and which I dared not reveal . . . and which, I am now sure, I never will dare to reveal.

IX

To live with life, without reasoning, without jibbing . . . letting oneself be captured by it . . . Not seeking happiness, waiting for it to arrive, from no matter where, in no matter what milieu, at no matter what moment . . . and when it's within one's reach, seizing it with a firm hand and not letting it escape, for it only brushes you once . . . But above all, live . . . live . . . !

Pierre must be right. I have been following his mental prescription to the letter for several days, but without expecting any relief. Since the dinner the other evening, my disillusionment and my confessions,

> *All alone, I suffer ennui, weeping*
> *And morose time sheds its petals;*
> *Slowly, like a rose,*
> *I sense my heart deflowering.*
> *All alone, I suffer ennui, weeping.*

He is exquisite, that Pierre, in counseling me to distract myself! But where, how, and in what fashion? He confesses himself that the riotous life is insupportable. So?

I don't want to see snobs, I don't want to see artists. I hate all those people, with an intense, ferocious, solid hatred. Snobs are unbearable, artists drive me crazy.

The only thing that still interests me is physical beauty, the beautiful human animal—at repose, of course. Clowns, gymnasts and wrestlers—outside the circus, for the odor of the stable and sweat make me faint with simultaneous intoxication and disgust. So, I go every day to install myself in the heart of Montmartre, near the cemetery, in a café next to a circus, and there I numb myself for hours, in a resolution of my entire being.

The interesting thing is the vision of an entire population of glabrous and bestial faces, with singularly twisted mouths: boldly cravated grooms, their legs outlined by deerskin trousers, with a stovepipe hat tilted over the ear; acrobats buried in eccentrically-colored macfarlanes, soft felt hats lowered over their eyes, and arrogant animal tamers and wrestlers, faces beaming, very "human flower," all at the disposal of whoever wants them, of either sex—and finally, clowns, very simply, poor clowns who are doubtless trying to forget the kicks in the derrière to receive that evening, playing an adversarial game of cards. I love that café of circus folk, where one can read in the faces of all the customers métiers of audacity, strength or skill; I love it for its appearance, half-boulevard café and half-fairground stall, for its odor of make-up and filth, for the conversations I overhear there, conversations in which the jargon of the métier returns constantly, like the chorus of a song.

"I had him well in hand after two circuits of the track . . . There's only Max who can bring off a reestablishment like that . . . It isn't the lion I fear, it's the tigress . . . You know that Gugusse[1] has sold up; he's giving up the struggle . . ."

Which is a change, and for the better, from the gossip at Maxim's or the Napolitain, and infinitely funnier than listening as an aperitif to Lucrèce Levy and his band of *lettraillons*.[2] And then, that entire population of circus folk charms me with its virility and gesticulations—especially the gesticulations. At times, in that society, there are hands that agitate strangely. They are men that one has before one's eyes, true men who run real dangers every evening, for whom a single moment of nervousness would be mortal, men who, for two or three hours before the eyes of an anguished public, will twist themselves around a fixed bar, a trapeze, or have exciting encounters with wild beasts. . . . In the meantime, they are there, in that bizarre café, tranquilly occupied in preparing their sugared absinthe and playing manille like good little bourgeois:

"Hearts . . . ! I win . . . ! Is it true that you've resigned for a month . . . ? Trump! Pique . . . ! I'm engaged in

---

1 Gugusse is a familiar form of the name Auguste, applied generically to clowns made up in a particular style, which then became generalized as an appellation for anyone playing the fool.

2 Probably a reference to the mythological painter Henri Léopold-Levy (1840-1904), nowadays best-known for a nude study of "Lucrèce" [the rape victim Lucretia famously depicted by Shakespeare], although it is usually attributed to a date long after the publication of the present story. "Lettraillons" is an improvised term implying trivial litterateurs.

Marseille for next month . . . Trump and trump again! Me, I'm not in the mood tonight . . . as long as I don't break my neck . . . Your deal . . ."

Hands shuffle the cards, feverishly.

In truth, they're very strange, all those hands. They have a life of their own . . .

One more corner where I roam in quest of emotion, the famous Emotion, which never comes any more, is the Rue Letort, in the waste ground scarcely a hundred meters from the Porte Ornano, in that quarter of leprosy and misery. Thirty yellow, green and maroon caravans sleep there, on muddy wheels, with zinc roofs invariably traversed by chimneys from which thin smoke rises. On the filthy soil, children of both sexes, angels and demons, boys with girlish figures and girls with boyish braces, fight and tear one another while rolling on the ground, pell-mell with starveling dogs and cats, lame, often one-eyed—and the whole society of brats, mutts and cats sing, bark and mewl while the women mend clothes—nameless rags—and the men installed at the foot of a caravan's steps play interminable games of find-the-lady.

"Come on, a little game! Put your bets down! Bet without fear, the merchant has enough to pay you . . ."

Sometimes—yesterday, for example, in mid-afternoon—when I was regaling dubious acquaintances in a nearby café, the turn of a card was contested, bitter words were exchanged, the discussion became envenomed, two parties formed, shivs and knuckledusters sprang from pockets and stilettos from bodices, and there was a horrible battle, men and women rolling in mud and blood, under the eyes of the kids and the dogs that came running, the kids to perfect their education as future professionals of nocturnal attacks and the dogs in the hope of a curée à la Jezebel . . .

And it is in such moments that I notice strange hands, veritable living chrysanthemums, which have the feverish crispations of petals.

Is the Phantom returning?

X

BILLANCOURT. The Phantom was materialized for me this morning, just now . . . and what an ugly materialization, what an abominable nightmare!

It was on the water's edge, at Billancourt, which I love and which will soon have loved me for ten years, at eleven o'clock in the morning, eleven *lead seals*, in Toussaint weather, premature for that languishing September, whether that reeked of damp sunlight and mud and blurred the bleak silhouettes of that suburban landscape—my perpetual hallucination!—that ragged landscape, the factory chimneys of Issy and rickety trees whose foliage looks as if it has been used to wipe dishes, the dream landscape of Huysmans' early work, in sum.[1]

---

[1] The principal reference is to Huysmans' prose-poem "La Bièvre" (1880 in *Croquis parisiens*), reissued in an oft-reprinted pamphlet in 1898. Jean Lorrain often quoted it, and frequently waxed lyrical about his perverse love of Billancourt. He wrote several stories about a sleazy riverside inn owned by Père Guillory, whose name is deliberately echoed by Fabrice. The Boulevard Exelmans and the quartier of Boulogne-Billancourt were within easy walking distance of the house in Auteuil where Lorrain lived in the late 1890s before

Billancourt! Weary of trailing my cravat from the tollbooth to the bridge, I went into the *Soleil d'or*, a low dive renting rooms for the night or a quarter of an hour, and when the landlord, Père Guillot, greeted me noisily I soon found myself being treated on an intimate footing by a gang of mates descended from Grenelle and Javel, or even from the terrible quarter of Boulogne, who were drinking absinthe and exchanging news of the Quai—their Quai, equivalent to our boulevard, the Quai de Billancourt, on which mugs picked up by the whores of the Boulevard Exelmans end up, mugs who have not yet been plucked, old rakes being weighed up before being lured with sweet talk down to the river bank, where lads are waiting with plugs of tobacco in their mouths and their hands in their pockets for opportunities to exercise their talent as drowners.

Abruptly, one of the mates recognized me, having encountered me several times in the establishments of Edmond Pézon[1] and other tamers, with my nose in a handkerchief soaked in ether and my eyes bulging before the central cage, eyes alert, desiring and waiting for an accident.

"You, here?"

"Yes, me."

---

moving to Nice in 1900.

1 Edmond Pézon (1868-1916) was a member of a famous family of animal-tamers. The image of a rapt spectator waiting for an accident to befall an animal-tamer is reproduced in two of Jane de La Vaudére's stories for *La Presse*, one of which was luridly expanded for reprinting in the *Lanterne Supplement* as "Volupté rouge" (tr. as "Red Lust").

And my memory placed Georges, alias Jojo, perfectly: a young fellow about twenty years of age, a carpenter in iron with velvet trousers and a thin moustache on a crapulent face admirably illuminated by two liquid sapphire eyes, like molten sapphires.

He interested me immediately, Jojo, who told me lewd stories in an argot devoid of coarseness, about his soft touches in the dance-halls of the Rue de la Gaieté, in nocturnal Montparnasse, where a chit who adored her little man worked for him on the Avenue de Maine. But, the demoiselle d'amour often being put away, cash became rare in Jojo's pockets, and the poor fellow would soon have been reduced to resuming his initial trade as a carpenter, as if that were not terrible for a fellow of twenty, a player, a vigorous chap, with eyes to light up all the amorous women of the banks and the slopes! The mates ragged him about that! All that Jojo had to do was dump his pullet and get another. Certainly, there was no shortage of kids, etc., etc . . .

Exquisite speech, was it not, of a very special flavor?

And as the mates were talking about going for a crust and Jojo, the desperate Jojo, was still lamenting the scarcity of money, I didn't hesitate to invite him to dine—but only with me—in a nearby inn arbor.

What a meal! First of all, to cut short the jeremiads, I slipped my guest a little money, and the latter recovered his joyful expression, in which the sapphire eyes had an infinite softness that I have only rediscovered since in the Louvre museum, in a portrait by Giotto, eyes of a simultaneously cold and ardent sensuality, the eyes of a poor

Nero. For he was not devoid of a certain nobility, that jolly rogue who preferred to go back to carpentry rather than change his kid!

After the meal we were smoking cigarettes when Jojo abruptly proposed to me: "What if we were to go to see Ma Pipe?"[1]

"Who's Ma Pipe?"

"You don't know Ma Pipe?"

"In truth, no."

"Oh, that's a pity. But it's necessary to know him. He's a delightful fellow, and he has a nice job. Today, the weather's good for him; he must be working at present. Let's go see him."

"Is it far?"

"Two minutes away, near the fortifs."

"What does he do?"

"You'll see. I'll keep it for a surprise. Only, you know, hush—necessary not to talk about what you're going to see. I'm taking you because you're a mate and I like you. Otherwise . . ."

We got up and made our way across the waste ground behind the guinguettes; and, as Jojo had assured me, two minutes later I perceived Ma Pipe and witnessed his singular work.

With the bottom of his blouse tucked into his trousers and his cap pulled down over his ears, his eyes attentive and his nose sniffing, on the alert, Ma Pipe was catching little birds, crouching in the narrow shadow of a hedge.

---

[1] This nickname translates literally, unsurprisingly, as "my pipe," but in Parisian argot—in which most of this chapter is cast—the verb "piper" usually refers to fellation.

He had strung his spider[1] between two trees by means of pickets, thrown down grain for bait, and the birds were fluttering around the trap, chirping.

He had arrived at daybreak, as usual, at that place, which he knew well.

"There's none better in all Billancourt," Ma Pipe assured me in a low voice, after Jojo had made the introduction, "and the birds allow themselves to be caught with great facility. As proof, the harvest: three chaffinches and two goldfinches."

It was only two o'clock in the afternoon. He still had the wherewithal, and more to do, provided that the flics didn't come!

Ma Pipe, an intrepid smoker, didn't smoke while he was working, or budge, avoiding coughing in order not to frighten the prey. Sometimes, he whistled, and his whistling imitated the song of a blackbird closely enough to be mistaken for it. Then, the wandering birds paid attention, and responded by chirping. They excited one another, for the song of the blackbird is intoxicating.

Suddenly, before my eyes, the vision appeared. The boldest of the birds, abandoning all prudence, lowered its flight toward the seeds that were scattered on the ground. Skimming the ground with its wing-tips, under the eyes of its comrades, it pecked . . . and *click!* The little net came down. The spider had done its work; the bird was captive.

The band of its brothers scattered in the gray sky.

---

1 In this sense, an *araignée* [spider] is a kind of net used by bird-catchers.

Then the man got up, came to the net, took possession of the songbird with his big hairy hands, and I felt a kind of frisson run through my body. An unspeakable fear, a terror, rose up within me.

I was afraid of that man, afraid of his hands, afraid of his artificial spider, and I fled, bewildered, as fast as my legs would carry me, before the amazed and alarmed eyes of the two men.

. . . There is an obsession within me that is growing by the day, by the hour, by the minute.

XI

SOCIETY and the Society of the Fête, I've been parading my melancholy in those milieux for three days. Women can't tolerate me. I'm inclining to misogyny. They're simpletons, for the most part, not to say all of them, from the young and old socialites who coo and cluck behind their fans, planning lush marriages and inventing sly gossip, all the way to the streetwalkers of the Bois and the boulevards, the demoiselles who sell vices that they don't have and are incapable of having. Oh, the false seekers of the absolute, the ladies who offer the strange at twenty-five or fifty louis a night!

I unmasked one yesterday, Edwige de Nancy—why Nancy, since she was born in La Chapelle, in the heart of a popular Parisian suburb? Those are things that one can never know. Because a young man has recently been discovered hacked to pieces, as the newspaper reporters put it, that unpunished crime is the object of all conversations and the subject of a few chronicles by neuropathic writers, haunted by sadism but very literary (a few cantharidic phrases but mostly rose-water), Edwige de Nancy has joined those who go to the Morgue every day to contemplate the poor mortal remains of the murdered wretch.

Every afternoon, the fashionable girly carriage stops outside the low and heavy administrative building, as if swollen by nasty grease, which is outlined against an ashen sky; and Edwige gets out, always accompanied by male or female friends, who report and commentate that evening on their visit to Notre-Dame-du-Suicide-et-de-la-Misère. She enters at an automaton pace, and without saying a word, places herself before the glass behind which the waxy flesh, brown or white—a liquefied white that is turning to verdigris—is sleeping the final slumber. And in that den of horror, entirely given to her memories, to begin with she smiles happily—at whom? at what?—and then, abruptly, tears run down her cheeks, tracing furrows in the make-up. Then, in the crowd of curiosity seekers, the rumor spreads that the luxurious lady who is weeping has just recognized some corpse, perhaps the young man hacked to pieces. People around her whisper . . .

But Edwige dabs her eyes with her handkerchief, and, cleaving through the crowd, followed by her friends, goes out stiffly, with the same automaton tread. In the evening, over aperitifs, at Maxim's, after the Palais de Glace, people wonder about what they call the passion of Edwige de Nancy. In that falsely corrupt milieu, nothing more is necessary to impose on the admiration of the snobs—and what snobs! Half clubman and a quarter socialite, the sons of enriched shopkeepers, all the little cockerels built on the same template, with the brains of apes and suits from good tailors, their hair parted to the left and the right from mid-forehead to the occiput, indulge in conversation in which the jargon of the sacristy, the barracks and the stable fraternize, to my eternal surprise!

I was so astonished when the macabre amours of the demoiselle were reported to me that I immediately wanted to meet her. And as my scandalous reputation, so nicely and so jealously entertained by my friends, and even by the indifferent, opens many alcoves to me, that night—last night—I easily became the temporary companion of the lady of amour, a pitiful temporary companion, but an agreeable talker, since we chatted for the greater part of the night. And what a dialogue! What confidences were exchanged in the depths of the alcove hung with Nile-green silk sewn with large white orchids, while Edwige de Nancy, sitting on the bed and rummaging in a purse, gave the impression of soaping her hands with sapphires and emeralds, sapphires as white and milky as drops of semen and as red as drops of blood, female sapphires of faded blue and male sapphires of the indigo of African skies, glaucous or honeyed emeralds, beryls perverted to whiteness—an entire profusion of stones, which the young person exhibited to me, knowing via hearsay of my passion for jewels and precious gems!

After the obligatory petty gossip, I brought Edwige to the chapter of her amorous pilgrimages to the bazaar of violent and anonymous Death. I hoped for and desired the revelation of some sadism, some perversity.

What dupery. Edwige was "normal," "very normal," sincere, not a trace of "tobacco-flower." She did not go to the Morgue in search of unusual sensations, to intoxicate herself with strangeness and vampirism. She went quite simply to pick the flower of family memory.

She told me that, since her early childhood, she had been accustomed to consider the Morgue uniquely as the goal for the walks for the Parisian poor. Many a time, her Papa and Maman, worthy suburbans, not knowing how to employ their Sundays—one cannot always go to eat ham sandwiches in the grass of the fortifications, and then, it snows in winter!—Papa and Maman took the little girl by the hand and went out, idling along the streets, musing at window displays, all the way to the sinister maisonette, the boutique of the dead, crushed and heaped up at the end of the Île de la Cité, behind Notre-Dame

"Well," Papa would say, disconcerted, "there are only three today. Truly, it wasn't worth the effort!"

And Maman concluded, sagely, that a walk here was better than going to the wine merchant's . . . and then, it was necessary to get some fresh air. "One can't always live imprisoned at home, caged like a brute. This distracts without doing any damage to the purse."

Accepting the idea that the Morgue was one of the agreeable places of Paris, the grown-up little girl, having become a streetwalker, who was nevertheless afraid, in her dreams of a demoiselle, of the idea of death, often turned in that direction in the course of an excursion, in order to come to see the Dead on the slabs.

That always amused her.

Now, as a woman launched in society, a favorite, in each of his voyages to Paris, of a royal prince, the latest crime had caused all of her past to rise up within her, and, careless of the scandal, perhaps even with a hint of blasphemy—who can tell?—she went to visit the cadavers as of old. In the Morgue, she communed *en famille*, wept over her past, for the blue dreams of her childhood, the candor of her youth.

And that was the lady whose sinister passion was cited by All Paris! A stupid sentimentalist!

Have I not reason enough to hate all of that society?

XII

THE obsession again!
Two o'clock in the morning. In my bedroom. It is scarcely an hour since I came back, fatigued by that Edwige de Nancy, even sillier than the others. I had not had any rest for more than twenty-four hours.

Thrown on my chaise longue fully dressed,

weary of vain sorrows,
And weary of lassitude,

by virtue of idleness, even of sickness itself, I had recourse to my Consoler, the one that never deceives me, Ether. And now I sense the firm and gentle pressure of a hand on my hands, like the cool breath of a calm night on my forehead, and at this moment, before my descaled eyes, in my bedroom, the ceiling of which is rising up and the walls retreating, my marble-tiled bedroom illuminated by white flames, a strange woman appears, tall and slender, singularly tall and supple. She is clad in a very simple dress of light fabric, of a shade mingling crimson and violet. The neck emerges entirely from the cleft, inclined in the grace of a charmer, her arm bare, outside of large sleeves, circled at the wrist by a bracelet of yellow gold with symbolic sculptures, her eyes half-closed beneath heavy brown eyelids, she seems to me to resemble an Oriental garden. Like a goddess of ancient days, in her hieratic attitude, she is reading the verses of the poet of Théos . . .

And, lulled by who words that are singing in her mouth, her mouth like a folded-back smile, I become a drowsy thing, voluptuous and fluid . . .

Then, my room vanishes. I am sitting at the extremity of a broad avenue of centenarian oaks, carpeted by thick grass, short and even, like a motionless emerald river, descending in a gentle slope all the way to a little slowly-flowing stream. Here and there, dragonflies are vibrating like minuscule rainbows, skimming the water, leaving on the liquid mirror the circular trace, quickly diffused, of their wings.

Spiders are lying in wait, alert . . .

The strange woman, so singularly tall and supple, is still there.

Tall? Supple? I sense, under that appearance, throughout her physical person, such an intimate correspondence, such a perfect harmony with her mental being, that I perceive sentiments and thoughts in the forms and in the lines. Yes, that woman has a Greek outline—the only outline that makes for thought . . . a face, of an exquisite, particular beauty of a perfect and complete eurythmia, fills the soul with a superior contemplation as well as charming the eyes . . .

But I know that face . . . it's . . . it's the face of the Dream, the face that always escapes me, suddenly fixed and incarnate, impregnated by and still vibrant with the ideal; it's the face evoked by me in all the museums in Europe, such that it appears at dusk, in the multicolored light of vaults, before the ecstasized eyes of Sanzio[1] when he meditated his portrait of the Virgin; it's the Beatrice, sower of roses, who held suspended from her lips the souls of Dante and Virgil.

How harmoniously my soul moves around that face!

. . . While I plunge my eyes into the luminous pupils, something agitates dully within me without my being able to grasp it . . . Yes, through my eyelids, closed now, her eyes are burning me . . . like a nightmare, their flames are wrapping around my loins the black velvet coils of the serpent of lust . . . for the apparition is naked now; I sense it . . . She is dancing and singing, the palms of her hands on her temples, to the bizarre sounds of derboukas and tambourines.

Why has she attached that singular gaze to me? Why do the words of her song have such troubling inflexions? Why is she proffering those bizarre phrases, the meaning of which I only perceive partially?

And yet my thought, like something dead in the cellar of my skull, reanimates under the influx of the life of those words. I have never sensed a similar power of speech on human lips . . . Oh! Is it drinking my heart sufficiently, is it pushing the ruby fluid in my arteries sufficiently; are the ideas circulating within me deafeningly enough?

The dance is speeding up . . .

---

1 Rafaello Sanzio da Urbino, a.k.a. Raphael.

※

I emerge from my past being as if from a formless chrysalis, from a nightmare that evaporates in my memory . . . a long grotesque and dolorous incoherence of dreams.

The dance accelerates more and more. It's a kind of Egyptian dance, a dance of culpable lust that agitates the belly, causes it to contort in the poses of intercourse . . . but the head remains cold and serene, maintaining a hieratical attitude . . .

In vain I struggle, in vain I evoke elevated and calming thoughts; the passionate torrent carries everything away in its troubled waves . . .

. . . Abruptly, a great, clawed red shadow descends from the prodigiously distant ceiling . . . Horror! I recognize that shadow; it is a Spider, a formidable spider . . . Oh! Now it is gluing itself gluttonously to the belly of the woman, and the belly, the poor belly is still dancing, agitating ever more feverishly, as if in precipitate sobs . . .

Everything around me is becoming disturbed now, and fading away: the perfumes, the forms and the sounds, and I only have the vague sentiment that it is there: the Phantom, the angel with wings of darkness that presides over betrothal with Madness . . . and that it is covering me with its shadow and pronouncing over me the words of a malediction . . .

. . . My ears are beating with a monotonous and liquid sound like that of waves, and gradually, I sense myself lying on the bed of a river, as if in a nuptial bed; and I sense the soft and gluttonous lips on my lips, things crawling over my entire body. Thus I roll, a pale wreck, in the ebon waves, and the plaintive murmur of the waters resembles the innumerable laments of all the dead . . .

. . . A ghoul is upon me, I tell you; she is crushing me, sucking me in with her tentacles . . . !

And when my submerged and vanquished eyes encounter hers, which open wide like gaping and profound amorous wounds, my body becomes as rigid and insensible as a cadaver, and I hear, flapping over our heads, I know not what standard . . .

And we are rolling, rolling, thus enlaced by the black river under a black sky . . . Fear, gigantic, supernaturally abstract fear, carries me by the hair into infinite space, without repose, endlessly . . . I wring my hands; from my mouth, convulsed by hideous laughter, a dull and continuous cry emerges, an inarticulate cry, a sort of extra-human expression of my thought and my being . . .

Who, then, hears the sobs? Who hears the cries, the supreme sighs and aspirations, of agonies?

✻

I have just emerged from the nightmare. Suffocated, I have opened the window with a moist and trembling hand, and for two hours I remain, shivering, under the breath of the night, weeping, weeping . . .

Oh, the torturing voluptuousness of tears, burning with remorse!

Eloi, Eloi, lama sabachthani?

XIII

For an hour of joy, unique and without return,
Preceded by tears and followed by tears;
For one hour, you can and ought to love life;
What man is not happy in his turn for at least an hour?

An hour of sunlight makes a whole day blessed.
And when your hand is subjugated every day,
An hour of your nights will still be envied
By the dead, who no longer have even one night for
amour.
      Sully-Prudhomme.[1]

THE hour of amour . . . I lived it this morning. Not an hour of amour in an alcove, or an hour of amour in a poet's dream, but that of my joy and my sadness, the hour of amour of my Paradise and my Inferno, of my Virtue and my Sin.

 I am intoxicated, abominably intoxicated by hashish, and I have departed again into the dream, far from the Phantom, the horrid Being from which I want to and

---

1 "La Joie," from *Les Épreuves* (1866).

must escape . . . And how dull and unreal life and the world appear to me when I compare them to my escape to the innocent lands of Dream and Fiction!

It is the vesperal hour, the gray hour when everything that is sensed dissolves. A pale sun rises on the horizon of the interior world, and bathes in its sheets of magical light the white terraces of an unknown city out there in the south of Oran. In the violet and transparent shade of oleanders, vague winged forms glide, which die away like melodies. It is the City of the Desert, only haunted by Spirits, the city that reflects its distant image in the mirror of the soul. It is the realm of marvelous marriages, in which the paranymphs penetrate one another and are unified in the blaze of unknown splendors, so that truth, beauty and happiness fuse into one and the same essence.

I want to stay here henceforth, in this reality, so white and so desert, in which I find myself entirely. I have lived the life and dreamed the dream of vanished generations, I have sensed the disgust of heaped-up souls, the disenchantment of mages, scholars and kings; and now I have entered into the heterogeneous legion of souls that have fled outside the world, in search of the ideal that slipped between their fleshy fingers down here. I want to live my life there, and nowhere else!

. . . Suddenly the strange apparition of last night looms up again, of the woman so singularly tall and supple. She rises up like a serpent stretching herself, looking into my eyes, her lips on my lips, and I feel the rigidity of her breasts on my breast . . . and now, by virtue of a bizarre transparency, she blossoms into an inexpressible and symbolic beast. Her body weighs ever more heavily upon my breast. She squeezes me and stifles me. The imprint of her mouth horrifies me. I feel the pressure of her fingers on my hands like soft viscosities. Her eyes resemble two large golden flowers . . .

My God! Her face is changing form . . . becoming triangular . . .

It's Her, Her, still Her!

XIV

TWENTY-FOUR hours of madness, of aberration, of departure for terror and death, because that Edwige de Nancy has not given my brain the hint of sadism that it demanded, for which it was avid. That is where we are, my youth and I!

All men bear within them a demon that aspires to become their master: Thought, that sixth sense! She has vanquished me forever, and I march in life with her and under her orders, submissive to her despotism.

> *The incarnate concern that lives in my soul,*
> *And follows me, riding on the rump of my horse.*[1]

What does the phantom want with me?

※

---

[1] Pierre Ronsard, "Complainte contre Fortune," reproduced (with the original archaic spelling) in volume six of the 1766 version of his *Oeuvres*, and in various nineteenth-century anthologies, and quoted by Gérard de Nerval.

Departure will be salvation, the sole remedy capable of curing me of hallucination and the madness that is yawning like an abyss beneath my reason and fascinating me...

Oh, yes, to depart, to flee my life! To travel the lands of my childhood, the Guérandaise peninsula, the nacreous salt marshes, the land of the people of my race, the land of salt where, in the shadow of Guérande-la-Figée, the delicate afternoons are gray, mild and exquisite in that epoch. Near the hearth, sitting on the bench, the old women mend the fishing-nets and the young mothers lull little boys with this song,

> *for which I would give*
> *All of Rossini, Beethoven and Weber.*

This melting song that weeps for Bretagne, my Bretagne:

> *Breton windmills are great birds,*
> *Which dip their wings*
> *In the secret of the waters;*
> *Breton windmills are demoiselles*
> *Turning and dreaming,*
> *To the kisses of the wind.*

And sailors returning from an excursion in old Saint-Nazaire spread out via Le Croisic, drinking coffee in inns, washed down with tafia, and then sing in chorus:

*The girls of the burg of Batz
With malice,
Laugh lon la, lon la lire lire,
Laugh lon la!*

And again:

*We were two, we were three,
We were two, we were three,
Embarked on the Saint-François,
My tra deri dra lon laire,
My tra deri dera lon la!*

And yet again:

*He has killed my white duck,
He has killed my white duck,
With his great silver rifle;
Let's descend from the darkness
My blonde;
Let's descend from the darkness
Of the woods.*[1]

Come on, lads, once more!

To depart—oh, yes, to depart and travel the coast, to "go to the sardines," to "hoist a jib" in the good company of all those sailors with seaweed eyes, slim waists and

---

1 The lines are adapted from verses of an old nursery rhyme, versions of which are found in England and Canada as well as France, variously known as "Le Canard blanc" [The White Duck] and "V'la l'bon vent" [Blow, good wind].

fresh skin . . . To quit this Paris of imbecile lust, which I hate, this Paris of excessive and artificial life, of nocturnal cafés where gypsies enervate me with the scraping of their airs of prey, those airs that empty me all the way to the bone marrow . . .

Depart! That's the "never, nevermore" that pursues me all day long, in the Petit Trianon where I stroll, a Petit Trianon whose grace, fainting, vanishes in a whirlpool of leaves falling in golden rain . . . and I retain the impression of having spent hours before a delightful pastel, a Latour, which fades away slowly, by degrees.

I'm taking the train tomorrow for my burg of Batz.

XV

I can't leave. It doesn't want me to leave. It's keeping me here, in Paris. It . . . Her!

Since yesterday, indescribable larvae of terror and horror have been prowling around me. What will become of me?

※

Here it is.

Gray-blue eyes, the sad eyes of an onanist in a triangle of saffron flesh eroded by chlorosis, still sweeping a thin mouth above a singularly curt chin. How immense and empty the forehead is! How discolored the little ears are! Black pearls are laughing in their lobes.

The face dances and prances, the cheeks ablaze like punch. She bumps into all the furniture, the tapestries and the ceiling, and always the profoundly sad eyes are spying on me, trying to enter into me. And then, suddenly, I observe that arms are snaking and stretching around the head, arms of darkness patched, in places, with crimson. Then the strange face is animated further, if possible; it swirls, and the legs that emerge from it writhe . . . It advances toward me, is about to capture me, to absorb me . . .

My God!

XVI

LAST night's terrifying dream: I'm still trembling with fear. This morning I got up shivering with fever. And that is where Pierre's prescription has brought me. Yes, it's the research of active life that his earned me that night of nightmares.

Yesterday evening, after dinner, weary of circus cafés and the leprosy of the fortifs, I wanted to try the music hall—not the Champs-Élysées music hall to which all the embarrassed demi-mondes drag themselves in October, all those who can't quit Paris for reasons of money or work, the demi-monde of letters, arts and the bank, of demoiselles without gigolos, journalists without "circulation permits," ruined clubmen and all the petty employees of finance and commerce; I wanted to try the old style music hall, which is to say, the pubic ballrooms, and I went to lose myself at the Moulin Rouge.

The Moulin Rouge! What odd types of both sexes one encounters there; insignificant and bestial vice, bourgeois vice, so to speak. It doesn't have the allure of high life, nor the bitter terror of base prostitution; the girls might be anyone—an anyone to make one shudder—and as for the men, it's rut at ten francs a night. How sickening!

So, I was wandering at random around the boring and bored hall, hardly distracted by the orchestra caged behind cast-iron bars above the crowd, or by stupid words, requests for beers and offers of beds, when a naturalist quadrille was announced, one of those that have made the fortune of that establishment of pleasures, slicing my attention. I moved closer, and it was then that I had a clear sentiment that the Phantom was still living in my shadow.

In a gray costume, as if sprinkled with dust, a thin being devoid of hips, with a clownesque face, giving the impression of slightly incurving liana: a very svelte being, in truth, a being of bizarre beauty and ambiguous sex, of a grace half mystical and half sensual, lifted a leg, leapt and contorted . . . oh, that leg, that foot, beating the measure, maddening in certain passages, that leg playing in a thicket of arachnean lace . . . and those hands, which clutched the hem of the dress . . . It gave me vertigo, rendered me crazy. It was like a dream of opium and ether rising up before my eyes.

How many joyous minutes did I stay there, gripped by nerves, indifferent to the stupidities of the surroundings—a host of imbecile sniggering strangers—how many, how many?

Abruptly, the orchestra fell silent, the legs were lowered, attitudes reentered into normality. The bizarre being with the strange gestures became a vulgar girl again, a Moulin Rouge dancer, scarcely agreeable. And as I looked at her at close range, this is what she remarked in a lewd voice, while drawing away on the arm of a friend:

"Do you see that client, Crevette? He has quite a gob!"

The ladies had passed by.

I quit the Moulin Rouge. I felt utterly sick. I took refuge in a café full of women, where former goose-girls and dishwashers were exercising the hard métier of gallantry. Then, even more rapidly disgusted, I got up and left. Outside, it was a warm night of the end of summer, a night cleft by raw artificial light. The silhouettes of helmeted hookers populated the external boulevard; in drinking-dens, Alphonse was playing maille. I advanced over the central reservation, my legs unsteady my gaze vague and my hands limp. The vision of the dancer had emptied me all the way to the marrow; I now belonged to that tilted body, that twisting leg wrapped in floods of ashen lace, like some great flower with a monstrous pistil.

After having wasted a few quarters of an hour in dives to which I was attracted by I know not what unhealthy curiosity, I searched for a cab, having decided to go home. It must be said that I was walking along the section of the Boulevard Rochechouart that is somewhat equivocal, between the Chausée Clignancourt and the Boulevard Barbès. Inelegant indigenes darted disquieting glances at me in passing, and continually, at intervals, strange creatures of sad nocturnal joys, streetwalkers clad in unspeakable rags, girdled by aprons, their necks emphasized by scarlet ribbons and hair over their eyes whispered invitations to me to embark for Cythera—great gods, what Cythera! A cab was definitely necessary.

And I was about to hail a marauding coachman with a sufficiently sympathetic physiognomy—for I distrust nocturnal coachmen—when an alcoholic landscape was offered to my eyes.

Perceived through glass, there was a high nickel-plated counter with a brutal glare, with men, women and children before it. How strange the twittering of those people was; how those mouths frightened me, which opened and writhed; how those hands hallucinated me, shaking one another, rising and falling. Some of them were trembling, to the extent of being unable to grip the glasses. Then the mouths twisted further and the hands, the poor hands, danced and danced . . .

Sinister, that alcoholic landscape! The sap that toils throughout nature, what power does it not contain! Without it, those bestial faces would never have offered me such bizarre puppets, such mouths howling with dolor, such thin lips with falling commissures. Oh, those advancing jaws. Those extremely prognathous faces, those lupine fangs beneath the brushwood of moustaches! And the eyes, the eyes! Nature has never furnished eyes like those, from the infinitely vague blue eyes, the poor weeping eyes of two or three old men, to the bulging dark eyes of a young Alphonse with an Apache cap pulled down over his eyebrows, dark eyes that gave the impression of wanting to spring out of their orbits and all.

Oh, that atrocious scream-inducing alcoholic landscape! But no scream reached my ears. Nothing came to me from that animate Goya, that Dantesque scene abruptly surged forth: nothing. And suddenly, I had the sensation of being before a terrifying and grotesque tableau, in the genre of those that amuse Parisian idlers—but a terrifying and grotesque tableau whose poorly-mounted mechanism caused arms, legs and lips to agitate in a disorderly fashion. Yes, the idea of a tableau with a mechanism running amok imposed itself on my mind, and I waited for the moment when the machine would break down, when the wheels and springs of the characters of luridly painted cardboard and wood would break and unwind, puncturing bellies and faces, leaping, leaping and leaping in mad capers.

I returned to the Hôtel Mordann, pursued by all those visions of dancers and drunkards, resolved to flee no matter what the cost; desirous of making my anguish cease, I tripled my dose of ether . . . and it was then that the Phantom came, escorted by an entire host of gnomes, saluted by astonishing flowers. Hallucination placed its clawed hand upon me, and deployed its fantastic arabesques in my mind.

That commenced with an abrupt stinging sensation of cold, which made me curl up in the bedclothes: a terrible cold that penetrated through all the openings of my bedroom, doors and windows alike; a cold that then, suddenly, made me get up and run, in order not to risk dying, frozen. How I ran, how I ran! The road stretched out, a thin, frail ribbon, so long that courage gradually abandoned me. I preferred the risk of dying of cold to that reckless and goalless race . . . for I recognized the road clearly; it was the one that connects the town of Batz to Le Croisic; but how it had grown, how it had stretched out like an earthworm . . . and now, in the cold night air, in which a thin white mist was drizzling, in which the mild odor of snow was floating, I was walking in a divine dream, in the luminous wake of a child gamboling before me, a child

who resembled me like a brother.[1]

I followed him, without thinking. Where had he come from? What was he doing at such an hour in that solitude? Was he the Child of the Sea, the legendary being whose cries of distress the coastal fishermen believe they hear on tempestuous nights, coming from the Plateau du Four? That question only troubled me momentarily, for I immediately resumed my passive assurance. That evening, my soul was stripped of its robe of sorrow. A new, happy soul had blossomed. It seemed to me that I was returning to the unconscious felicity of the old days, the dead days, in which I had not yet traced the separation between myself and the "self" that frequented the boulevard, theaters and solons, running around the spas and the disreputable streets of ports and Grenelle, when I conformed to the law of life, ignorant of Vice, when, in sum, I participated in the unconscious and solemn vegetable enjoyment of being . . .

Vegetables! Their august placidity penetrated me; my soul, purged of doubt and problems, deployed such foliage and flowers, in its primitive almost unconscious faith, and the very idea of death, the idea brought forth

---

[1] A line from Alfred de Musset's "La Nuit de décembre" (1835), in the section subtitled "Le Poète." The poem repeats the line several times, like a refrain, as Fabrice does in the story, mingled with other lines from the hallucinatory poem in question.

by the vision of the open sea in the gulf at my feet, was enveloped by verdant hope, like antique tombs, living and flowery depictions.

The child was no longer in front of me now, but behind me. I sat down on a block of granite above the beach of the town of Batz, and he came to place his hands over my eyes, playfully. While his youthful laughter, sonorous and pure, burst out over my head, like the song of a nightingale, I felt the pressure of his fingers, like roses in my flesh. The sensuality of that contact, by which I was impregnated, lasted for a long time, like a slowly evaporating perfume.

Suddenly, the Breton vision vanished. I found myself back in my bedroom, prodigiously illuminated. Farfadets were playing behind the blinds; swarms of elves were passing in procession over the drapes. The room became extremely sonorous; whispering voices were murmuring vague things. Then came a gasping profusion of crazy and nervous czardas, rhythmed by castanets and the clatter of the sandals of a battalion of blond ephebes devoid of hips, with rounded torsos and no loins . . . and all the music and all those dancers fled into the thickness of the wall!

Once again I found myself alone in my room, this time before my looking-glass. It sent back my image, and also shadows; one of those hollow and idle shadows, shadows of light souls that do not haunt the torment of infinite space, nor anguish, nor remorse: shadows that formed a flock led by the child of a little while ago, the one *who resembled me like a brother.*

He had grown up, and grown old. He displayed an elegant vice of the most recent fashionability . . .

And all those figures spoke to me, invited me to excursions in the dark suburbs, into the fantastic palaces where somber fêtes were held . . . and I followed them, and penetrated with them into those dives in the depths of Grenelle, wine merchants' halls in which red curtains over the windows hid monstrous priapisms from the eyes of passers-by, and scenes of bardashism in which heavy and vigorous cuirassiers mingled with a battalion of blond hipless ephebes, ephebes returned in a glory of music, light and flowers . . .

And the shadows dragged me away again

into charming boudoirs with flowery hangings,

and there, I finally found all my own people, all my soul-brothers, those who, like me, had something to kill. On their faces the regal stem of Vice was resplendent. I sensed that they were followed—just like me!—by specters that followed them like dogs. And all of them were fleeing themselves, and all of them, in order to flee themselves, were hastily emptying phials of transparent liquid, like rock crystal. Ether! Ether! That was the consoler, the great friend that gave them strength, that put all the pariahs to sleep, them and me, all of us whom sleep has deserted, for whom Hope is ungraspable—Hope, the livid prince who bears on his helmet, wings deployed, the black vulture known as the Chimera.

And then, once again, everything suddenly died, everything fell into silence around me. I had returned to my bedroom, but my bedroom was astonishingly bright, white and cold. I closed my eyes. Gripped by vertigo, I felt myself sinking into a hideous light, a brightness of unpolished glass that, in spite of the crispation of my will, attracted me like a prey. My personality dissipated. As if in a sky heavy with storm-clouds, the beloved visions, the few beloved visions, fled, grimacing like ironies. And beneath my closed eyelids, my pupils lit up like blazing windows.

Under the vault of my skull, which was amplified like a gigantic cupola, incessantly growing, the rumps of Sin and Vice raced, whirling under an infernal symphony in which I recognized in passing Chopin's *Funeral March* played as a waltz, mingled with the airs of belly-dances. Sniggering goats, their eyes purulent with lust, quivered and howled voluptuously. The muzzles of strange animals bellowed. Apocalyptic beasts combining the features of spiders, bats and lizards, fluttered heavily. Hairy hands unattached to any body, kneaded the breasts of Byzantine virgins. Long cadavers, tinted violet and green, swung regularly from the arches of windows, amid the hum of large golden flies. Headless bodies shed their blood here and here, like great inverted amphorae. Satyrs clicked their tongues. In the shadows, filthy arabesques, like serpentine knots, convulsively coiling their viscous rings. And now squids with multiple arms and multiple mouths invaded the room, sucking plump chimeras mortally.

Then the Child of the first nightmare, the Child

who resembled me like a brother

surged forth, and I perceived that he was formed of all that was impure in all the animals of the earth. He was crouching on a golden pedestal, wearing like diadems seven blasphemies on his suddenly-septuple head . . .

I woke up. Corpses surrounded me. They were everywhere. On the sofas, in the armchairs, on the floor, lying on the carpet . . . so many corpses! It was the peaceful hour when the interior specters were paralyzed in brains saturated with poisons, when, before the troubled eyes of my soul-brothers, the obscene sabbat passed like a convulsion, which made a blissful smile flourish on all mouths . . .

And I woke up, alone, lucid, in a petrified meditation, while, her breasts naked and her face pale, grimacing amorously, the dancer from the Moulin Rouge leaned over my forehead like a Medusa and murmured in my ear:

"To efface your pale specters, go toward the red specters of crime . . ."

Maddened, I hurled myself upon the Child

who resembled me like a brother . . .

The Child had appeared again as he had appeared in his first incarnation, svelte, pure and weeping innocence, and with my fingers making a necklace around his neck, I squeezed . . .

Then the Child's head was detached from his body; it suddenly changed form, became triangular, became the face with the sad eyes of the onanist in its saffron flesh: the face of the Phantom strix whose feet I could hear undulating and tapping beside me all night long . . .

XVII

TWO letters this morning.
One was from Louisette, tender and sweet, bringing me news from Carlepont. My mother and my cousin are quite well. One point; that's all—an "all" expressed in the prose of a schoolgirl who adores the herborist Theuriet.[1]

The other was from Pierre de Nidine, inviting me to a voyage by automobile and railway, not to mention patache. Yes, those dear friends are quitting Paris, for two months, in order to travel in Switzerland, three days in Interlaken, a week in Lucerne, twenty-four hours in Berne and returning via Geneva-the-Hypocrite, not forgetting a night in Fribourg, Fribourg and the salvation of evening in its cathedral, the playing of the organ celebrated by all the guide-books . . .

Switzerland! A land I detest, with the beauty of pan-

---

1 André Theuriet (1833-1907) was one of Lorrain's fellow-members of the *Journal* stable, contributing a weekly item to its front page. Theuriet's contributions mingled fiction and non-fiction in a kindred fashion, but were far less "decadent," heavily biased toward nostalgic reminiscences of childhood and studies of nature.

oramas painted by Poilpot[1] and other spoilers of canvases, artificial Switzerland, graceless for my Breton eyes amorous of my Black Mountains and my sea, disliking the imbecility of falsely wild locations.

And yet I shall go; I shall travel in the company of that charming household; I shall seize in flight this opportunity to flee Paris and my hallucinations. By means of sunlit roads, skies in fête and verdures eaten by light, I count on losing the suggestive faces that have populated my head since the evening of my trip to the Moulin Rouge. Yes, next to my friends, in the amiable conversation enjoyed by those lovers, it will surely be possible to find a little happiness for me. I don't even demand happiness, but only calm.

We leave tomorrow, at dawn.

---

1 Théophile Poilpot (1848-1915), a pillar of the academic art of the era, painted panoramic scenes, especially of military history, very few, if any, of which depict Switzerland.

XVIII

He has departed, the one I love,
He has gone far way from me
He has departed, grief extreme
And he will never return.

THE obsession of that tune, moaned by all music boxes, imposes upon me without my being able to drive it away. I find it again everywhere, in all the streets, chalets, casinos, facile ascensions . . . what am I saying? I even find it on the singing lips of Madame de Nidine. It is the ridiculously old-fashioned ballad of this land of Opéra-Comique scenery—an Opéra-Comique with scenery not organized by Jusseaume.[1]

Switzerland! I believed that I would find there, if not happiness, at least calm, in the company of the Nidines. I hoped that the pleasant vision of the loving couple and robust kisses that sing clearly would bring me back to normality. Vain hope! Their cheerful words, their laugh-

---

[1] Lucien Jusseaume (!861-1925) was a celebrated theatrical decorator and designer, attached to the Opéra-Comique after 1898.

ter, their fashion of wanting to make me a third in all their joys, the continual invitation to gaiety, enervated me from the start. Scarcely had we left Paris than my friends wearied me. That same evening we slept in Dijon and I began to hate them. Yes, hate . . . Why? Because at dinner, in the couple's amicable teasing, I read that they were only tolerating me out of pity; they were distracting me, as one distracts a poor fellow momentarily, out of pure goodness. I've said the word: *out of pity*.

And I don't want to inspire pity.

The night, especially, was terrible. All the happiness that I brushed, the kisses that seemed to be singing in the next room, hallucinated me. Who knows whether these false friends are not dragging me with them in order to heighten their joy? All night long that nagging question infiltrated me, posing its question mark in my poor head in my despair. And when, in the morning, a hotel maid came to warn me that I was awaited for the departure—a rather pretty hotel maid who knew well enough how to wake travelers—I went to find the Nidine household, well furnished with that fine hatred.

It only grew throughout the journey. Those people associated me with their thrills, their embraces and their languorous kisses, a whole viscous display of souls in love, the continual speech between lovers: *Tecum vivere amem, tecum obeam libens.*[1]

I've had enough of it, truly, enough of the vision of all that happiness; and sometimes, when one or other

---
[1] "With you I should love to live, with you I would be ready to die." The quotation is from Horace.

of them wants to rehash their passion, sarcasms rise to my lips. Twice I was on the point of asking them, in a bitter tone, whether they were making use of me as a stimulant.

So, this evening I'm quitting them, after only eleven days of this communal life. I'm quitting them on the shore of Lake Geneva, as flat and cold as a stupid watercolor by Hugo d'Alési.[1] I don't even want them to take the funicular to see me on to the train at Lausanne station. Let them stay with their amours, let their enlaced silhouettes irritate me no more; and above all, let them not treat me as an invalid to be pitied.

Don't those two simpletons understand, then, that their pity enrages me?

---

[1] "Hugo d'Alesi" (Frédéric Alexianu, 1849-1906) was a prolific painter of posters for railway companies designed to attract tourists to various destinations.

XIX

Down the drain.
 I've become the unconsoled solitary again, the taciturn wanderer whose gaze is turned inwards, whose soul, curled up like a wounded sensitive-plant, is seeking the interior expansion of consolatory ideas. Two days ago I returned to hashish—in vain; I can't succeed in abstracting myself, for the Phantom is there, and I sense it prowling. It has insinuated itself like a subtle fluid, all the way to the ideal refuge of my obsessed soul, and I'm very clearly conscious that it's gradually transforming my medications into deformed dreams.

But what indescribable struggles! My hands become moist, my body is covered in cold sweat, my legs buckle . . .

※

Had aperitifs at Maxim's and dined at Amenonville in the company of merrymakers and demoiselles. Those puppets! I always astonish them by composing the black scenario of nocturnal orgies, creating new varieties of perversity and intoxication and mixing philters of vices and virtues. If they knew that I am, alas, only an actor of debauchery, always conscious and tortured beneath the rictus of my mask . . . !

※

A trip to the Folies-Bergère, which has just been renovated, a cigar on the Boulevard, an appearance at the club, where I left a few louis, and at one o'clock in the morning I found myself in the heart of Paris in fête, near the Madeleine, alone and tearfully sad.

I picked up two poor girls who were returning, heads lowered, to the Europe quarter, and took them to supper. I gave them money and put them at ease in order that they could stun me with the lewd talk and the filth that rose naturally to their mouths. Finally, I got them drunk—but they could not give me a single minute of quietude.

At times, when coarse laughter shook the dazed stupidity of their masks of drunken idiots, I tried to enter into the rhythm. Wasted effort. My feigned gaiety froze theirs. It was like a black cloud staining a white sky. Their laughter melted into grimaces.

And then, it was then that the Phantom, prowling around me but not showing itself, loomed up momentarily in my eyes, with its triangular mask. Yes, it is always watching, constantly beside me, and I sense its grasping hand in the shadows. It never quits me; it's there, as faithful as a sword.

And all that evening I sensed it sliding between my flesh and the delicate and perfume-saturated skin of the women. It even expanded into their smiles and swam like a shadow under the surface of their pupils.

It is also the Phantom that, in the wan daylight, in the middle of the boulevard, at the exit from the Americain, while I was putting the girls into a carriage, anguished me before a muscular hand, brightly gloved, its fingers clutching the carriage door—a hand like a white spider . . .

XX

A week of excursions, follies and fêtes, a week of music halls, the wings of petty theaters and café-concerts, a week of suppers and insane sensualities, and returns to the Hôtel Mordann when dawn extends idly in a sickly blue sky.

And the Phantom is still there. It delivers me to ridiculous fantasies, makes me play the revenant with the unfortunate whores that I drag into night cafés.

Playing the revenant! It's quite simple. I cheer the demoiselles up with the aid of a few louis and champagne, I make them laugh and sing, and "have fun," as they say, and when they have gaiety in their eyes, when the joy of living shakes their lifeless flesh, I suddenly talk to them about their family, I cause their childhood to reawaken. They always had a little brother who died a long time ago, when they were little girls, or a grandmother or an uncle . . .

Then I lead them gradually to make the memory of the death precise; I harass them with multiple questions; I evoke the dead person, raise him over the women, who are troubled, go pale and dissolve in tears . . . Oh, my pleasure in seeing those masks capsize, those eyes flooded with tears, big tears that run in trickles, tracing furrows in the white grease, rouge and rice-powder . . .

I know that what I'm creating is the absurd, the unreasonable, but I soothe myself with the thought that at least, for a few hours, I'm not alone in suffering the phantom of my childhood.

The tears of one of those whores, above all, were delicious to me.

Three nights ago, I went down to the edge of the quivering water near the Auteuil viaduct, and, moved partly by ennui and partly by curiosity, I went into an open air concert-hall poorly sheltered by canvas and palisades.

On the rudimentary stage, in naively ridiculous scenery—a doorless drawing room, a landscape of disconcerting hues—overly mature ladies, lamentable clowns, appeared one after another, abominable under their make-up, faded and withered demoiselles, all the rabble of petty actresses and streetwalkers that one sees grouped at the doors of the sleazy cafés around the Porte Saint-Denis, the poor band of singers at three-francs fifty a day, dinner included.

And all of that was bellowing, mewling, laughing, cooing, accompanied by a piano as hoarse as an old drunk, and it unleashed laughter and amused appreciations from an audience of workers, mariners on the spree, dubious individuals in blouses, with the eternal caps pulled down over their eyes, like livestock dealers, perhaps apprentice milkmen . . .

It was lamentable, but droll, and above all intoxicating: all the surrounding joy and all the ludicrous or admiring exclamations that departed like rockets from the bosom of the audience. It took on substance by virtue of the atmosphere, the indefinable odor of verdure, running water, sweat, alcohol and perfumes at nineteen sous a bottle.

I stayed there for an hour, glued and numbed by the charm, before an execrable meal, smoking excessively dry cigars, in a slightly flashy entourage—but what did it matter? The joy of the audience, healthy and loud, had conquered me, much more than the sinister faces of the fatigued, broken down actors and actresses, with the bruises of their over-carbonized eyes and the bloody wounds of their excessively rouged lips.

I was about to retire when a frightful girl appeared on the boards, tall, thin and lamentable; stringy blonde hair was fluffed up over the forehead between the temples, a rascally gaze filtered from the yellow eyes between abominably blue-tinted eyelids, the thin-lipped mouth was slack, the chin receding—the insignificant face of a faubourg whore.

Sheathed in five meters of flower-patterned liberty that gave the impression of having been carved into a dress from a pair of curtains for a maid's bedroom, flat-chested and long-legged, the singer advanced, addressed a queenly bow to "her" public, which was stamping its feet with joy, and the gurgling ritornelle of the drunken piano began to vomit a gigantic military drinking song. Her cowherd voice displeased me and I was getting up to leave when one of her gestures gave me a shock.

Breathless, I sat down again.

It was because her hands and arms, gloved in crimson—but imperial crimson, as if steeped to the elbow in a bath of blood—were agitating so convulsively, contorting in movements that I knew well, too well; I no longer heard the singer, I was indifferent to the audience, I no longer saw anything but the hands, which were still "knitting," trying to imitate the gestures of a tourlourou imagined by the comedian Ouvrard but ending up shuddering like a spider's legs.[1]

Oh, those red hands, those monstrous hands, opening and closing, those feverish fingers, those phalanges elongating and curling up again in an entire aerial reputation; those hands, doubtless soft and doubtless cold, which gave the impression of departing into the void in search of prey; those blind hands that were groping and seeking to grasp; those tentacular hands that writhed, wanting to suck the emptiness—and with that, red, abominably criminal, fingers like the arms of an octopus . . . those hands, those hands gorged on blood!

The vision disappeared, the girl was replaced by a marloucratic baritone.[2] I emerged from the concert, terrified.

Outside, there was Stygian darkness, the tragic bank, the purring, soporific river, the feline river that promised

---

[1] Eloi Ouvrard (1855-1938) was a famous café-concert performer who composed countless comic songs, celebrated for his invention of a genre of *comique troupier* [soldier comedy]. A tourlourou is a kind of crab, whose oblique gait Ouvrard imitated in some of his "dances."

[2] The obsolete word "marloucrate" and its associated adjective, referred to the power exercised by Parisian pimps over their whores.

kisses and enlacements, with glimmers on its skin, was enclosed by a décor of nightmare and the Apocalypse. The street was desperately inky.

Abruptly, surging from the darkness, aureoled by the raw light of a gas-lamp, an aged flower-seller was before me, with a basket over her arm, an odorous basket of roses, teasing me with the offer of her services . . . what services!

I saw that she had a "ready for anything" appearance, which gave me confidence. I bought some flowers, asked the name of the singer with the red gloves, and dispatched the old woman with hard eyes, a honeyed voice and seductive gestures to the girl, in order to tell her at the end of the spectacle that a monsieur was waiting for her in the Boulevard Exelmans, on the viaduct, in a carriage.

Two hours later the singer was sucking crayfish in a bar on the Rue Royale, joyful at having received ten louis, and slightly astonished by the fact that I had greeted her, when she came to join me, with: "Do you have the red gloves?"

"Yes."

"Put them on, then."

If she had not had the red gloves, I would have sent her away.

So she was sucking crayfish, putting on airs, glad to have found a "genteel fellow," as she put it, and seeing her position assured. But the red-gloved hands were no longer singing to me. They had only fascinated me when seen with the mirage of the boards. Now, they only appeared to me as they were in reality: vulgar, clumsy hands devoid of breeding, the gloved fingers of a dish-washer.

When the girl was high, drunk on champagne and poultry—the poor thing had devoured half a chicken, perhaps not having dined—I drew her on to the terrain of familial confidences, more, I admit, out of idleness than vice; the hands had spoiled my habitual enjoyment . . .

And I made her weep a few minutes later—yes, weep like the others—as soon as I had evoked the phantom of her childhood and her child, the brat that she had had at fourteen, a sad kid spewed out at eight months, a kid for whom her family had chucked her out. She wept abundantly, sobered up by those memories; she wept and wept . . . The rascality had disappeared, her voice was veiled; in the waterside hooker I had just resuscitated a scarcely-pubescent child and an entire dolorous childhood, a childhood well-buried, well-hidden, well dead. She wept, and wept . . .

Honestly, no tears had ever moved me as much as those! I was sure that I had reawakened in the soul of that whore a Phantom that would not fall sleep again, a childhood as eternally dolorous as mine.

From that night on, I sensed, there would be someone in the world who was suffering as much as me.

XXI

"FUTILE to search, Monsieur, you won't see her again. She's left the Grand Neptune . . . it was the day after the evening when Monsieur took her away. She left suddenly, giving as a pretext that she was going to her kid's grave. You can imagine whether the comrades were pleased . . . and the boss . . . when she didn't come back. I was the only one who suspected the truth, but I don't talk . . . not often . . . I said to myself: Monsieur has shown her a good time and the brat is the excuse she's giving for going on the spree. Well, Monsieur, have I guessed right? Because, you, Monsieur, don't believe the story of the kid either . . . that's a joke! Can you see that girl— who, between us, is a real slut—suddenly remembering that she has a kid buried somewhere in the province and rushing off to go put flowers on his grave? What rubbish, eh, Monsieur? Come on, Monsieur, believe me, you're young, you gave that kid too much dough. When one wants to be sure of finding a woman again, it's necessary not to give her too much dough . . ."

And the flower-seller, outside the door of the concert-hall, to which the obsession of the red gloves had brought me back, shook her head grotesquely. Then, as I stood there, indecisive, as if broken down by the news of the abrupt departure of the singer, she continued:

"Of, if Monsieur cares to tell me what he's looking for, I can surely find him kids entirely to his taste, and better than singers. Not decked out like princesses, of course, but with figures and eyes and pretty little hands and lovely hair . . . genuinely young, of course . . . and healthy . . . girls who've been brought up on the river bank, at Billancourt. Monsieur has only to come and see and he can give me news of them. All afternoon I'll be at a nice little bistro called *Au Clown de l'Hippodrome*, on the towpath, before you get to Jeanson's. Come and see me there, Monsieur, and I'll show you young things as fresh as roses in that house of fun."

Sickened, without replying, I threw the woman a silver coin, who smiled with her yellow eyes, and I fled, not without still hearing the flower-seller barking at me: "*Au Clown de l'Hippodrome*, Monsieur. I'm there all afternoon . . . making my bouquets."

I returned directly to my house.

So my urgency was not misplaced. The singer with the red gloves was now dragging the cadaver of her childhood. I had the joy of knowing that someone else was suffering my malaise, but also the regret of seeing one of my joys abolished. The red hands by means of which I wanted to escape, the red hands that by means of which I might have escaped, the monstrous spiders gorged on blood that had only lived for ten minutes for me, were holding me under their domination.

Four days have gone by since the evening when I took the girl to supper. And during those four days her memory has remained there, installed in my thought. Her gloved hands, which, in the restaurant, had become indifferent to me—almost antipathetic, even—her hands gradually reappeared to me under the first impression that they had given. I saw them agitating convulsively again.

They were haunting me!

They were haunting me, yes, but their haunting might be able to cure me, for I knew where to see them again, stretching and twitching. I could satiate myself with the intoxication of their vision, and satiety leads to disgust and indifference. By dint of seeing the spidery hands I would arrive at finding them grotesque—and then, my renascent passion for the insects would vanish. I would liquidate my folly for spiders. I would triumph over my puerile and cruel soul.

But the girl has gone! Where? No one knows. She has left for the grave of her child, the poor mother whose ignoble executioner I have been. She has departed, taking away my hope of a cure.

Have I been punished cruelly enough for having made so many tears flow over so many dolorous childhoods?

XXII

WILL I be delivered from my malady?
I think so, for after the fortnight of prostration that followed the adventure of the singer with the red gloves—oh, who could describe my anguish and suffering during that fortnight, my excursions in the city, wasted evenings squandered in music halls, circuses and even fairgrounds in search of other hands that I have not seen?—now, suddenly, the Phantom has created another fantasy for me; a remembrance has risen within me, an old amour has reflowered: I am giving myself entirely to flowers. All the pink roses and all the white roses are scattered profusely in my room, my study and the large drawing-room of the Hôtel Mordann.
Flowers . . . flowers . . . they will cure me; that's certain . . .

XXIII

FLOWERS ... flowers ... !
One might think that wide eyes are gazing at me in all the rooms in the house. Perhaps it is only me who is projecting that indefinable expression into their profound and changing pupils? With amazement, I repeat to myself that I have never known such gazes ...

And then, those wide eyes speak. What are they saying to me?

I know that they have been speaking to me for a long time, but I can only find in my memory a very clear and purely musical succession, which repeats, like a refrain, the word "amour": a modulation sometimes slow, like a prayer, and sometimes intermittent, like sobs, which I don't understand and of which I don't then sense all of the heart-rending expression.

These flowers!

How their eyes create a void in my brain and expel any other preoccupation but themselves! What a singular power they have acquired, at length, over my mind! I stand before the roses for hours without saying a word;

and I sense, head bowed, eyes fixed upon me obstinately, which burn me. Oh, the frissons when I raise my head!

At those moments, I dread seeing them, all the eyes of the roses, carnations, dahlias and chrysanthemums, which are aimed at me so obstinately. But I can no longer flee them. They possess me. They always shine before me, incarnating in their infinite changes of expression and color all the forms of my thought, as well as the rare possible joy that frightens me.

This evening, in the abandonment of the Hôtel Mordann, huddled in the depths of an alcove over a book, where I compress my forehead, circled by my clenched hands. I saw them blossoming gradually, like wilted flowers with incessantly renascent petals.

Again, in my study, where I take refuge, strange eyes are incarnate in the calices of all the flowers. Oh, the eyes of emerald, topaz, ruby and sapphire, which develop in the soil and on the side-tables; and above all the eyes as white as angels, which float in the mist, the eyes of lilies! Like candles at the bedside of a dead man, their flame palpitates over my forehead all night long.

The flowers . . . ! The flowers!

XXIV

HOW it toys with me, the Phantom! It has made me depart over the flowers, has given me illusions, and now, again, my hopes are going down the drain. Oh, that cruelty, the need for refinement that ravaged my childhood! It's like a rotten orange that has slipped, by accident, into a crate of healthy fruit. I am corrupting all great ideas, all noble sentiments, all the beautiful things that live or exist around me. My new and innocent passion for flowers has not escaped the contagion.

For these days of brown October—sun and rain, half-ill weather—at Bas-Meudon near the water, I had rented a little white and mauve house, an elegant and cozy little house whose gardener had embellished it with the joy of blooming roses, arabesques of chrysanthemums and the candor of an unfamiliar scented species of lilies that only flower in autumn—the whole of that little garden in blue shadow, scarcely striped with the gold of rusty foliage, under a sky of mauve silk with pink reflections. Everything in the house was lilial: carpets, drapes, furniture; a true courtesan's house. It pleased me; it was a change from the Hôtel Mordann, where the servants have too many beaming smiles.

So white, that little house, and so white my fluttering dreams! My being, until then in limbo, truly awoke amid joy, light and beauty. In the midst of sprightly flowers I lived, radiantly. Nothing any longer tempted me. The curiosity of insects, the temptation of the spider, was dead. The thirst for the sensation of the contact of skin, for music, for color and vice, was dead.

Oh, the beautiful return to innocent childhood, innocent and so jolly!

But I compromised that joy very rapidly. And I compromised it because I wanted it to be grown up again, more refined, because within innocent childhood I awoke cruel childhood: it sleeps so little!

And for several days, in the garden and the little greenhouse where the sun laughs at tears, here and there, over the somber green of leaves patched with rare, bizarre, delicate and violent colors, which are flowers, I have been and am becoming anxious, pushing a little cart laden with bottles, phials of medicaments and instruments of a surgical appearance.

Around me I have concentrated all the strangeness of a deformation or a perversion of nature: black lilies opening thin mouths; red violets displaying gigantic petals, enormous orchids unhealthily white; jonquil hortensias as big as children's heads; monstrous tulips and mousy irises; all the terrifying splendor of atrophy and hypertrophy.

Oh, the sad joy of living here! A frightful malady is undermining me and making that new mania turn, so to speak, to tragedy. By means of cutting, separating and injecting those plants with various products in order to make them produce flowers of different colors, I have acquired a taste for murder. *I torture the flowers!*

Leaning over them, I pour little drops of violent poisons, which make them die slowly, very slowly; some, like orchids, have petals that flutter, which one might think were flapping wings; and, my eyes bright, my hands clenched, and my respiration halting, I watch and rejoice in their agony. I am recommencing living the joyous minutes of Noyon.

What abominable being am I becoming? Two days ago I brutally tore apart, petal by petal, all my red violets. I kneaded them between my fingers and rolled them into little balls, and the juice that ran along my hands resembled a thin and frail ribbon of blood. Yesterday, I burned lilies atrociously, large lilies in all the majesty of their expansion; then I tried to care for their burns. I surrounded them with minute cares. Most of them were dead this morning, but some have survived. Those bear in red stigmata the traces of their suffering. And what other dolors await them tomorrow?

Where am I going? How far will I go?

XXV

IT came back last night.

It leaned its triangular face over me and pronounced my name passionately. In the caverns of its eyes, two changing flowers were shining. All its life seemed to be converging there that evening like an ardent hearth. And, looking into its eyes, what extravagant meditations I made on the rich and metallic colors of the Iris! How they absorbed me, how I plunged into dancing vertigo in the depths of its large profound pupils, like wells. Anguish was wrung in tears from its eyes, drop by drop, like an infernal sand-glass . . .

And then, suddenly, my head was so close to its face that my lips stuck to its mouth in an unconscious kiss . . .

Its mouth! It blossomed, a red flower, in a supreme smile that death suddenly fixed on its lips. From its eyes soft flowers in rings, strange flowers sprang forth, sprang forth . . .

Finally, the eyelids closed, the face became an impassive and cold mask, seeming to savor the unusual sensuality of death . . .

It departed.

XXVI

AND the flowers have brought the spiders back to me. My old passion has been reborn, more ardent and stronger than ever. It was the dahlias received from my gardener that earned me that awakening of the old evil.

Yes, it was the enormous dahlias, dahlias that cast a bloody note into the accumulation of multicolored carnations, sheathed in tender green, mauve and blue orchids elegantly outlining prints by Sosen[1] and Hokusai, and blue cockscombs, it was the dahlias that threw me back into the insanity of spiders. In truth, yes, as enormous as balls of wool, the center of each black petal, the back of clotted blood, the fine petals curved back toward the middle and twisted, the dahlias were similar to large funnel-web spiders with a thousand legs. When the gardener had left, I remained on the path in front of them all afternoon, frightened, not daring to flee; they held me under their charm. Several times, in vain, I tried to escape the spell and draw away from those accursed flow-

---

1 Mori Sosen, like Hokusai, was a Japanese painter much in vogue in *fin-de-siècle* France, best known for his paintings of monkeys.

ers, but a force greater than my will—inertia—held me there, and I stayed.

But the dusk was troubled by a violent gust of wind, the precursor of a storm, which abruptly ravaged the garden, causing the trees to quiver and decapitating plants; one of the enormous dahlias was separated from its stem, and its bloody head rolled along the path, fantastically. The vision was animated. Oh, yes, it really was a hideous funnel-web spider that was running toward me, all its legs projected forwards . . .

Panicked, I ran into the house and bolted the doors; howling. I ran from room to room, in the dark, for I sensed it on my heels, the beast, the spider; it was surely running over the floorboards, climbing up the curtains . . .

Then, suddenly, a great calm came over me; I traversed more rooms; then, cunningly, I closed the doors, went downstairs and double-locked the main entrance door, my entire being shaken by a ferocious little laugh that I did not recognize, and I abandoned the house; I departed into the night.

I had locked my terror in the house!

That irrational idea imposed itself on my mind. I tried to expel it, to find it absurd, but it came back, acutely. And the little ferocious laugh shook me again.

I walked all night, at random, aimlessly, in the Bois de Meudon, ravaged by a frightful storm, and in the morning, covered in mud, my clothes in tatters, I found myself near the pond at Villebon, still sniggering . . .

I went back to the Hôtel Mordann.

XXVII

THE HÔTEL. My mother and Louisette, rediscovered, are installed here and preparing to spend the winter here, Maman is not going to Nice this year. All three of us will remain huddled in the old town house.

"Elsewhere," says Maman, with a thin smile, "it would be necessary for me to economize. I'll have so many expenses to make in spring!"

She is alluding to the marriage that she desires, the union of which she dreams between Louisette and the big lad that I am. Since my sister's marriage and the death of my father I have observed that an evolution has taken place in Maman's character She, who still only wanted to live as a socialite last year, whose sole preoccupations related to frippery, seems today to be essentially concerned to ensure the position of her son. She has a presentiment that I am incapable of defending myself in life, and it is for that reason that she wishes to give me a reliable guide and counseler—and Louisette appears to realize all her desires.

Every time there is mention of that marriage I smile, embarrassed—much more embarrassed than my cousin, to whom Maman must have imparted her projects.

It's just that the idea of marriage is so distant and so foreign to me. A few months ago, I was perhaps still "marriageable," but today, when I am suffering from a strange, indefinable malady, when I have awakened in myself an infantile cruelty, and in trying to make it disappear and go back to sleep, I have, on the contrary, made it more robust and more powerful, when my heart is swollen by abominable desires and equivocal enjoyment, how can I accept to mingle a young woman with my life?

That thought crops up twenty times a day in the course of my meditations; it installs itself at my bedside in the morning, does not quit me all day and still pursues me in my nocturnal dreams. It is that problem of conscience, which I dare not resolve, which keeps me in the house, preventing me from running around the city, where everything, in any case, must be sad and black in these November days steeped with rain—muddy, morose days of depression and vague sorrow.

I have resumed my cloistered existence in my room. Lying on the floor, on cushions, in front of the log fire that is singing in the fireplace, I smoke tobacco bizarrely mixed and powdered with hashish in small red pipes—my famous pipes once purchased in Oran.

And I depart far from the present life, I resuscitate the Past. I depart for countries in which we have lived, at the caprice of my father's garrisons, for the Algeria of gold and ocher that melts and burns, white Tunisia, almost chalky, that dazzles; I see again long, broad plains of golden sand that the blue sea bites, ringed in the distance by lilac and pink mountains, as pink as oleanders; then, passing Arab houses similar to huge gaming dice that seem to have fallen into plaster, domes like half-oranges that have followed them there, and towers and terraces, and bizarre streets, and the corners of caravanserais where minuscule donkeys are somnolent in the heavy evening, and kneeling camels under the guard of grave camelteers as serious as diplomats, while big saluki dogs repose, their muzzles extended between their forepaws; and I go astray in a maze of back-streets; multicolored fabrics, carpets and trappings to which the sun attaches threads of gold hanging in the atmosphere where odors of amber, musk and benzoin linger . . .

There are covered passages, stairways hooked audaciously on to dazzling walls, and more streets, and more passages, and more stairways. At intervals, groups of indigenes with coppery faces—but a copper that I remember having been daubed with soot—repose indolently, crouching in the shadow of a gallery, the perforations of whose fronton are clearly outlinded . . .

And there is still a dazzle of color, there is the bizarre music of derboukas, and landscapes into which sunflowers and palm trees put a hint of freshness, and the immense plains that the sun kisses voluptuously . . .

And it's all of "Africa" that surges forth again for me; the mysterious Africa, the land of domes, terraces and colonnades, the superbly sad land of tarnished enamels, with its white and powdery streets of sand, where the art of vanished races is expended without measure; it is "Africa" that is evoked, phantasmal, sordid, magnificent, prodigal, poor and dirty—but a blonde, gilded dirtiness, in rags that shine and are not the rags of the Occident; and it is an entire life, fifteen years behind, that I "see" again in the room where, curtains drawn day and night, the paintings, books and furniture are illuminated by the golden light of a candle with a jonquil lampshade,

Oh, that exquisite fortnight in November, the hashish that puts to sleep, poisons, and kills the nightmares of last summer!

XXVIII

Have I been stupid enough, staying throughout the month of November in a sad room, brutalizing myself by smoking hashish, when life is so beautiful in the street, on days when the sun wants to show clemency?

This morning's walk—what joy! Adorable weather: mild, a sufficiently gray sky of exile—the mild sky of exile of my Bretagne—which make it unnecessary to regret the blue sea and skies of the Africa that still drew me into my worst divagations yesterday.

And how enchanting the infinite Boulevard d'Italie is, broad and not at all hostile, in this end of autumn that veils and blurs all the houses, sidewalks and trees! Oh, the good wanderings, the exquisite early mornings, the smiles of the housewives, the rubicund faces of the coachmen and the sallies of the Parisian workmen!

It is necessary to be as ridiculous as I am to deprive oneself of all that, to go to earth far from life.

Life! It intoxicated me this morning. I came home for the morning meal drunk on movement and good health. The cure is certain now. I've found a remedy, and it's . . .

a butcher-boy who has furnished me with it. This is how it happened.

I was prowling the sidewalk, alarmed by the animation of an ambulant market, interesting myself in the arguments of maids and petty bourgeois women, glad to be in that noisy crowd, which was crying out gibes and the prices of goods, to be in that atmosphere flourishing with greenery and fruits, when, troubled, I bumped into a stout butcher-boy who was circulating in the crowd with a basket balanced on his head. The butcher caught the basket in time but I expected to endure a volley of insults. To my great surprise, the boy joked:

"Nice—a little more and the meat would have fallen on your noggin."

I saw laughing eyes in a round face, pink and plump. I apologized.

"No harm done," said the other. "But if you were a dear, old chap, you'd help me get my basket balanced again—the pad is slipping down my neck. Here, grab the end!"

Unconsciously, I obeyed. The butcher replaced the basket on his head and continued on his way; and, in truth, I followed him, attracted by that jovial face and the pink flesh, full of health, of the muscular arms that emerged from tucked-up sleeves.

When the little market had been passed I offered him an aperitif.

"On the go, then?" the boy accepted.

And there we were, at a wine merchant's counter. The vermouth absorbed—"on the go"—we departed, chatting with the familiarity of old friends.

"You don't give a damn, then?" exclaimed my new acquaintance. "Lucky you! I'd like to be in your shoes! I'd have a good time . . . always getting around, always on the spree. You'll only find me on the streets of Paris, a plug in my mouth and my feet in the gutter. All the same, it would be nice to stroll around all the time and breathe the good air. Ah, lucky man!"

The boy's eyes lit up at the thought of "strolling." During the two hours that I spent in his company, wandering through the quarter, that idea of "strolling" returned constantly to the conversation, and was gradually implanted in me. When I took my leave of the butcher I had found the remedy for my anguish: strolling.

So I promise myself to stroll all the time now, amid people who are busy. In contact with that toiling humanity, I'll find energy and strength—virility, in a word. I'll become a man. And I too will have muscular arms and pink flesh full of health!

No, it's truly necessary for me to be stupid to have spent so many years rotting in solitude, dragging my plaintive precious person from a chaise longue to an armchair, when Life is there, the Life that makes one strong and happy . . .

XXIX

THE cure is succeeding. Honestly, if, a few months hence, I'm not a male in the full meaning of the word, it'll be cause for despair.

For a week I've been taking lessons in wrestling and I'm learning to juggle with dumbbells. Charming!

In the course of one of my morning walks through the intoxicatingly noisy faubourg, I made the acquaintance of Charlot, the Terror of the Gobelins.

On the Boulevard de la Gare on Christmas Eve I approached a gathering, attracted by the need to rub shoulders that pushes me into crowds. And abruptly, as soon as I was in the circle of idlers, I was subjected to the sadness of the lamentable music of a barrel-organ. It was a slow and mournful modulation with outbursts of false notes and the agonized sighs of trailing notes, an exasperating song that afflicted the nerves with a bitterness full of vague things—an unhealthy impression, against which I had difficulty reacting. I elbowed my way through in order to see. It was a matter of fairground strong-men! There were two of them; one of them, in particular, was very masculine, with a powerful, stocky torso, broad shoulders, a strong head on the neck of a bull, ink-black eyes in a bestial face, but which did not lack character, and hair "à la chien"—I almost wrote "à la Polaire," for the black tresses covered the forehead all the way to the eyebrows.[1]

In the middle of the space left free on the ground was a sordid, colorless, threadbare carpet, surrounded by weights and dumbbells, all the poor equipment of a performing strong-man. In a corner of that arena, the organ was being ground by an old man. Sous were thrown on to the carpet, but it appeared that a sum of forty centimes was lacking, for which the messieurs consented to juggle weights, after having "regaled" us with a bout of wrestling.

Comments on those things were buzzing in my ears, emanating from that good and worthy audience of soldiers, laborers devoid of work in peaked caps, plastered whores, the inevitable telegraphist and the no-less-inevitable patissier. The décor was simultaneously very Chocarne-Moreau and very Raffaelli—that depended on the intelligence and the eyes.[2]

"Come on, Messieurs, a little courage, a little courage . . . eight sous are still lacking, eight shells . . ."

---

[1] The briefly-popular hairstyle known as "à la chien [*sic*]," adopted by Polaire and becoming an aspect of her image as distinctive as her famous "wasp waist," was so-called because of its supposed resemblance to a fashionable way of shaping the hair of poodles.

[2] The painter Paul Charles Chocarne, alias Chocarne-Moreau (1855-1930) specialized in slightly cartoonish scenes of Parisian street life, often featuring patissiers. Jean-Francois Raffaelli (1854-1950) initially specialized in more realistic images of the same street life, controversially exhibiting alongside the impressionists at the invitation of Edgar Degas; his work was praised by Joris-Karl Huysmans.

But the shells did not fall, and the two pink leotards were wasting their time. One of them, the one with the Polaire hair-style, threw a jacket over his shoulders and put on a soft felt hat—and thus clad, was quite bizarre and very equivocal.

I felt sorry for him; I threw six sous and I fled, for I anticipated lamentable exercises. Why watch them, then?

Involuntarily, as I strode along the Boulevard de la Gare, I made comparisons between the two plebeian fellows I had just had before my eyes and the company of free men who conquered immortality and golden crowns for the amusement of the Sovereign People in an immense circus hung with golden nets and splendid awnings, in which lions and panthers roared and a hundred thousand spectators were seated. Oh, what had become of the real and bloody dramas, the ferociously moving encounters of Thracian slaves and Sarmatian and Gaulish prisoners, struggles in which the vanquished fell, struck by the victor's sword, the mirmillon's gladius or the retiarius' trident!

Instead of the immense stone terraces known as the Coliseum, whose lists were sprinkled with cinnabar and golden sand, there was the Boulevard de la Gare on a foggy morning in December, the bitumen soiled with filth, with an entourage formed by male spectators in coats and caps and female spectators with flesh corroded by infamous make-up, for fanfares of trumpets the lamentable voice of a wailing barrel-organ, and for athletes, two butchers banished from the stall, one of whom had the hairstyle of a girl!

An hour later I found myself before the two pink leotards again. They had begun a new "bout." They still lacked those forty sous . . . I threw them the forty sous. That caused a sensation; all gazes converged on me, and in spite of my boldness, I was slightly embarrassed.

"Good, nice—the cove isn't tight!"

"For sure!"

"He seems to like the hercules!"[1]

"Perhaps he makes use of them . . ."

"He isn't windy!"

The two-franc piece having fallen, the man with the Polaire hairstyle got up, his gaze fixed on me, and there was a kind of pass of arms, two adversaries feeling one another out with the buttons of their foils. Under the irresistible seduction of the golden dots that blazed in the ink of the quivering eyes, my eyelids lowered, and when I opened my eyes again he was beside me, very close, his hand extended for me to give him mine.

"Why, it's you," he said, nonchalantly, like someone rediscovering an old acquaintance with whom he had lost touch.

I made no response, slightly alarmed by that familiarity. I smiled. He continued, with a familiar gesture:

"It appears that one's flush, eh? It's nice to help the mates out. But you're amazing—a double louis on the

---

1 The trivial noun "hercules" was a common term employed for fairground strong-men. By the turn of the century Jean Lorrain had become a notorious connoisseur of such individuals, unashamed to be seen in public in their company, much as the Marquess of Queensberry liked to exhibit himself on the fringes of London society in the company of boxers when he was not busy fitting up Oscar Wilde.

carpet; that sets an example for the rabble . . . one understands that it's a down payment. We'll meet later, eh?"

And the acrobat beat a retreat, while his companion proclaimed: "Messieurs et Mesdames, Charlot will commence the exercises. Play the music!"

The barrel-organ wailed. Charlot commenced the "exercises." First they were twenty-kilo weights that he swung with a certain grace, then dumbbells with which he played, throwing them up and catching them in midair, to the thunderous applause of the public, interested to the point of enthusiasm. Finally, "Monsieur Polaire" lifted a two-hundred liter barrel full of sand . . . oh, that last "exercise . . . !"

His back braced and his chest sticking out, his arms stiff under the terrible burden, he paraded his gaze around the audience without a single muscle in his face quivering, and slowly, the golden gleams in his eyes stuck like birdlime to my eyes, penetrating and seductive. And I was caught, swallowed, absorbed by the gold of that gaze. An entire health, a good humor, a sound life was transfused into me. An exquisite enjoyment! I sensed that he would not let go of the weight, maintained by his wrists a few inches above his head, until my eyes were satisfied. A vertiginous emotion gripped me. I took a bitter pleasure in prolonging the voluntary torture. I wanted and did not want the burden to crush the man, in order that that health, which I envied, might fail, in order that that body, which I would have liked to have, might be broken . . .

Oh, yes, let him keep the heavy barrel at the end of his arms for a long time, let him not weaken! I had no pity for his torture. It was necessary that he suffer . . . Still high, the weight was still high . . . still, still, always . . . !

Cries buzzed in my ears:

"Enough! Enough! Let go!"

The anguished public was afraid. It wanted the spectacle to end.

"Enough! Enough!"

Charlot did not let go. He looked at me. His eyes were ablaze. Large drops of sweat were pearling on his body, running down his forehead and cascading over his face; his neck and his breast were streaming above his back. The hercules was out of breath. The burden was crushing him.

Oh, my enjoyment was so cruelly sweet!

Terrified, the crowd howled: "Enough! Enough!"

But he found and continued to find unknown strength in his undaunted body, and he did not let go . . .

And it was only at my smile, and an unconscious clap of the hands—a fit of nerves that drove me to applaud in order to calm my irritation—only at that mark of my satisfaction, or, at least, what he took to be a mark of satisfaction, that he dropped the heavy mass.

Cheers burst forth; in the blink of an eye sous strewed the carpet, while the barrel-organ wept bitterly again in its shrill voice—that poor voice, which breathlessness sometimes transformed into an agonized death-rattle.

And from my inner depths a regret rose, that of not having allowed the handsome fellow to be crushed under the burden for a few seconds more, in order to enjoy his inevitable defeat, his shame at the moment when the weight would have reckoned with his muscles, when matter would have vanquished the animal, the gross animal, the beast that lived in the body of the athlete, the beast that I would have liked to live in me, in order that the tortures of my mind might be stifled . . .

After that day I no longer quit Charlot: Charlot, who held me under his charm, like a familiar dream; Charlot, whose special mask filled me with joy and frightened me at the same time. I am only seen in the Hôtel Mordann at meal times. The rest of the time, day and night, I spend in the strange company of athletes and wrestlers. I am one of theirs. Charlot exhibits me proudly, as his worldly pupil, to his "mates." We run around taverns from Grenelle to the Place d'Italie, arm in arm; sometimes I return home blind drunk, having partied too much with the gang: Totor de Montparno, Biscuit des Gobelins, Fils de Soir de Montrouge and others, others that I forget, all fairground artistes, all ruffians, and without prejudice, all thieves . . .

It seems to me that with them, I recover health and good humor, that it would collapse in solitude, and that without it, I would perceive "the spider I have in the ceiling," as my comrade Charlot sometimes declares, when he sees that I am sad, without suspecting the exactitude of his metaphor.

A murky, crapulous life, which calms the conscience.

XXX

THE river-bank! It is in that strange company that I run it, that I allow myself to be gained by the dangerous charm of the modern landscape, that raw décor in which the only mild and soft note is provided by the water. Oh, these skies of ice and soot, these low skies soaked with rain, the hallucinatory face of this twentieth-century Paris, these factory chimneys plumed with multicolored smokes that flocculate or stripe the sky brutally, these low walls, these baldly paved river banks, and the water above all, the special water of great cities, green and yellow, as if bitten by vitriol . . . !

The banks of the Seine. It is, in truth, all the life of the great city at work, colored panoramas of Paris unfurling under colored skies, with the brick-hued factories of Charenton or Bercy, the dead stones of the Quai d'Orléans in the Île Saint-Louis, where, above the walls, tall windblown trees make phantasmal reverences in large noble and solitary gardens, and, silhouetted on the horizon like vast Chinese shadows, the Arc de Triomphe and its graceless mass, the Eiffel Tower like a gigantic candlestick, the flattened golden dome of Les Invalides, and the two bewildered arms of Notre Dame reaching toward the street, and sometimes Sacré-Coeur, all pink, Sacré-Coeur as pink as an oleander, reminiscent of a gigantic caravanserai . . .

Below all that, the leaden water sometimes takes on the hue of evil absinthe and molten emerald—the water that always reeks of fever and fear . . .

XXXI

THE river-bank! I made very equivocal acquaintances last night out there, near the Pont de Grenelle, aboard a barge to which I had been taken in order to party by the band of "mates" in the company of whom I roam.

In that low room, that cube of plants that reeked of tar and salt, a dozen individuals, waterfront idlers with bright eyes in the faces of freshwater pirates were dancing the Java,[1] the dance of the worst faubourgs, with young rollers of hips like women in the blue velvet jackets dear to riverside workers. The scene was worthy of Heliogabalus and Henri III, and that got on my nerves somewhat . . .

Then, in the unfailing drinking that accompanied that debauchery of gestures, a popular song continually recurred, intoned by a pretty blond; a song that will now always remind me of last night, evoking it forever . . .

---

1 The Java was a kind of fast waltz, often danced while the male partner placed his hands on his partner's buttocks, which led to its being banned in more respectable dance-halls, but many music hall songs were composed to accompany it. It was new when the present story as written and did not reach the peak of its popularity until the "roaring" twenties.

Last year at the Neuilly fair
I made the acquaintance
Of a solid and well-made fellow,
The greatest tamer in France!
He had big doll-like eyes
Of such a tender blue
That my heart has been stolen
By that solid and sturdy chap![1]

And the chorus went:

He's so chic in his cream costume
That I swear to myself
That he'll be my one adored
As long as he stays the same.
I have the tamer in my blood!

Then the verses continued:

But you ought to see my lover
When he tames his wild beasts.
He's chic, he's amazing
And always wears a mauve iris.
I love him, he loves me, we're happy,
We embrace all the time,
And then, he's so amorous
That I'm mad for the crack of his whip!

---

1 An original work that has much in common with Jean Lorrain's poem "Fleur de berge," although the latter is not addressed to an animal-tamer.

> *We supped with the men of the Bois*
> *All well-mannered types.*
> *And I'll live for a few months*
> *With my tamer near Asnières!*
> *That will last as long as it can,*
> *And when I've had enough.*
> *Paris will see me again,*
> *Drunk on amour and worn out!*

And with that, as everyone laughed, the pretty blond told us, crudely, the origin of the music–hall song, the argot-laden declaration of a man of letters currently in vogue, to one of the animal-tamers of Paris, the most costly in the demi-monde. Then, his bag of gossip empty, the singer passed from hand to hand.

What a culpable night!

While returning to the Hôte Mordann in the morning, just now, my carriage crossed the path of the Nidines' auto, which was carrying the amorous couple along the Avenue de Versailles. I turned my head swiftly in order not to see the happiness that I hate.

Oh, how I hate them! I hate them because they are simple and entirely kneaded by amour; I hate them with a fine and strong hatred, because I'm a "complicated" person who hasn't conquered his happiness, who will never conquer it. I hate them as civilization hates savagery. I hate them . . . with an envious hatred . . .

XXXII

ELEVEN o'clock in the evening, at the Bal Mouffetard, in the cabaret that precedes the dance hall.

At a greasy table, three men are playing cards under the suspicious gaze of the municipal guard. Those three men are Charlot des Gobelins, Totor de Montparno and me—me, at table with those bandits, one of whom, Totor de Montparlo, is wanted by the relegation!

That is the strange, the absurd, the equivocal company into which my desire to return to the candor of my childhood has led me! Oh, that need to live a robust, agitated life, a "male" life, is it martyrizing me enough? And yet I found happiness and quietude again under all that; but for a few days my conscience, momentarily calmed, has had awakenings and shocks that worry me; I sense that the Phantom is still there behind me, ready to seize me again at the slightest weakness. It has not released its prey; it is observing me. If it catches me again, where will it drag me? Into what unfathomable abyss will I fall? What crime will the enjoyment of cruelty that has awakened in my soul of a petty assassin make me commit? What spider will torment me . . . ?

In order to flee those ideas, I shall definitely no longer party with the mates. For three days I have not been back to the Hôtel Mordann.

What must Maman and Louisette be thinking? And if Maman, frightened, has the police search for me, what will she think when it is revealed to her that her son is on a footing of equality and camaraderie with the assassins of the Place d'Italie, Vaugirard and Grenelle? What if she is told that he prowls around behind the military school and on the Boulevard Garibaldi, and the terrible Boulevard de la Gare, where the agents find a man lying face down on the ground on an hourly basis with a shiv between his shoulders; if she is told that he roams in the company of flat caps, check suits, velvet trousers and blouses, that he has been sleeping for three nights in the "pad" of Charlot, the Terror of the Gobelins, the kid with the lovely locks, as the whores call him, all smitten with the sturdy fellow, the whores that only speak to me in a tone of hateful mockery? If she is told about those scandals, what will she say, my poor Maman?

Oh, these thoughts, these thoughts that obsess me! Better to play cards.[1] So I play cards.

Announcements of quadrilles, polkas and waltzes rise from the ballroom. Then, from time to time, there's a Java, the crapulous dance in which men swing their hips

---

1 The word I have translated here as "play cards," *cartonner*, has numerous other meanings; it might not be irrelevant that it is sometimes used as a euphemism for sexual intercourse, in the same way that another possible meaning of the French verb, "cover," is sometimes used with respect to livestock breeding in English. It can also be related to equivalents of the English euphemistic phrase "in the closet."

like whores. The customers get up, quitting momentarily the bowls of warm wine and the tankards, and the entire population shakes, turns, twirls and embraces; all the girls with clustered hats that bounce on their heads to the beat, all the lovers of "pigeon wings" and even lads whose eyes one might imagine to be magnified by kohl and whose lips are painted, lads dressed in first communion costumes, quadrille, waltz and polka to the sound of a frightful orchestra: a trombone, a trumpet, two bassoons and an ophicleide—out-of-tune instruments that vomit an atrocious music.

Oh, the ignoble popular tableau that has nothing in common with other popular tableaux of other countries! Oh, where is the Greek *cordace*, gay, lively licentious, but witty? What has become of the bacchanals, the amorous dances that painted delicately the actions of marriage, all the pleasures of ancient Rome and emperors, of that youth of enviable virility? Where are the visions of gypsies dancing in the dazzling enchantments of light and harmonious intoxications . . . ? No, this evening, it is the dancing of the posadas—blossoming in flowers of lust to the sound of nervous guitars and mandolins, with castanets clicking like bursts of sadistic laughter—the whirling of gypsies rolling and undulating in a hectic flutter of ragged muslins in the feverish launch of maddened legs, which only offer themselves passively, because they are exhausted, to the man—or perhaps to the woman.

"Well, what more do you want?" Charlot asks me. "You're lost? That's because your spider is working on you! I've been waiting for ten minutes for you to drop the queen of clubs." And, turning toward Totor, he adds:

"It's true, he's terrible, this chap. He must surely have a spider in the ceiling!"

"I know what you mean," mocks Totor, "but you know, talking of spiders, I saw one at work the other day, with Rodolphe le Boucher. Oh, they work hard, spiders!"

And, as he doubtless took note of my agitation, after having winked, he added, while drinking furiously: "For sure you, although you know traveling folk, have never encountered the Spider Man. That name's one in the eye for you, eh? He's an extraordinary fellow, and I've never seen such amazing exercises. Even you, Charlot, have never done anything as pretty. Oh, it's necessary to believe that I'm showing you the greatest of trainers of performing insects. Everyone knows that the work of fleas, or lamberts, is a joke . . . but the Spider Man, I tell you, has no peer. Imagine a tall, thin fellow with bizarre eyes—round green eyes, you know, frog's eyes with a big gold patch in the middle, true frog's eyes. I tell you . . . and his paws, you have to see his paws, I tell you . . . hands that can't keep still, which move and elongate, truly, like spiders . . . It disgusts you to sense them close to yours and to shake them, slackly, hands whose fingers one would think were grabbing yours. And with that, a sad fellow, all alone, never any tenderness or fun, always drunk, a phenomenon, my friends! But when one is completely wrapped up is when he works. This is what he does . . ."

And Totor mimed.

"He begins by putting a little box in front of him, on a table. He opens the box and takes out a flute and plays it. All that's routine, no? It's the rest that's terrible. One sees emerging from the box, one after another, two large spiders, all red, with a hairy body, spiders larger than my thumb. Naturally, the public, before that spectacle, is a bit scared There are even gonzesses who faint in the corners, especially when the spiders walk, running on their feet. They advance to the edge of the table, and then, abruptly, they let themselves fall to the floor on the end of their thread, and there they are, climbing, climbing after the man, who crawls on his hands. One would think they were two red pearls or two drops of blood. Then the fellow throws away his flute; he takes a big living fly by the wings and he presents it to them. Oh, I tell you, my friends, what happens! There they are, the two spiders, who fight, who jump on to his skin, who try to kill one another, I tell you, and all that in the hand of the Spider Man, who presents his paw as a platform, as tranquilly as milord offering a lottery ticket. But what's the matter with you?" Totor adds, addressing me. "You're trembling, rolling your peepers . . . are you mad?"

My pulse is beating the retreat in my temples. Predatory forms are whirling around me. My eyes cloud over. And I hear imperfectly Totor pronouncing, in his indefinably mocking tone: "Oh, his eyes are spinning. I tell you, Charlot, he's more nervous than a gonzesse, your mate! Well, you know, he has a funny way of celebrating New Year's Eve. Patron, vinegar!"

XXXIII

THAT lamentable New Year's Day!
I can still see myself collapsed in an armchair, and I can still see Maman and Louisette fussing around me, putting pillows behind my head, attending to my blankets, swaddling me like a baby.

I was sitting next to the window in my bedroom, and I could see the snowy décor of the Boulevard d'Italie and the Butte aux Cailles—oh, yes, a white décor, a candid décor, for that first day of the new year, the trees, the ground and the buildings that surround our house dusted with frost, all that under an Arctic sky, a sky the vision of which chilled me to the bone, gave me frissons, a sky from which an invincible sadness fell, condensed into invisible flakes.

Oh, that sky of the first of January, the silence of that atmosphere, which hung inertly, having become perceptible, and all that foggy life! And the Boulevard d'Italie, more sinister in that ermine mantle than its black mantle; the boulevard where even the foreground was blurred, where all the silhouettes were anguished by vague and profound apprehensions. Something unexperienced floated there, only comparable to the fears that certain dream landscapes cause. A strange malaise, a cold sadness, gripped my heart.

Oh, was it snowing enough bitter ennui, was enough incurable desolation falling upon that tableau bordered by my windows?

In my capsized mind, like an old tune forgotten for a long time, returned and singing shrilly, there was the lassitude of interminable desolate days in which, the head empty and the heart inert, one seems to be traversing an endless plain, shivering in an impenetrable fog, in a rhythm of crises, when the obsession, the spider with the quivering legs is knitting with a feverish activity around imprisoned thought . . . And always over that accursed theme I collided with unprecedented terrors . . .

The past of the previous day surged forth again. There was Charlot, Totor, the band of thieves and my crapulous life of recent days . . . Let's see, was I dreaming? Did all that really exist? Was I not the victim of my diseased imagination? Had I really gone to the Bal Mouffetard the previous day? And the Spider Man, his hideous "work" described by Totor, was that not a nightmare, a horrible nightmare? And my loss of consciousness, my crisis of nerves in that dive, my return to the house, sustained as far as the door by the two bandits, my silhouette of a collapsed drunkard—had that really existed?

Yes, it had existed. I saw myself again ringing at the gate, shouting: "Help! Help!" and falling into the arms of the domestics who came running, half-naked. I saw old Yves again, who was my father's valet for such a long time, Yves, who raised my sister and me, Yves, who is almost a member of the family now . . . I saw old Yves carrying me like a child in his still-robust arms up to my room, laying me down on my bed, undressing me with tremulous hands, checking to see that I wasn't wounded . . . I can hear his emotional voice again reassuring my mother and Louisette, who had got up in haste and run to my bedside.

"It's nothing, Madame . . . Mademoiselle . . . Someone has simply robbed poor Monsieur Andhré . . . he no longer has his watch, his rings or his wallet . . . but . . . but . . . it's nothing. Don't worry. He's alive, he's alive . . . there's no harm done!"

And after that it is black, it is night, a leaden sleep . . .

The next day it is New Year's Day, so white, so white . . . Doctor Fauvières at my bedside, calming Maman and my cousin . . . and the whispered advice of the good doctor . . . so good but so closed to the maladies of the mind.

"Marry him . . . marry him quickly . . . that big lad must have been gadding about . . . the proof, Madame, is that you've told me that he hadn't been home for several days in succession. He's bored . . . he must have been in search of amorous adventures . . . and has got himself robbed! Marry him, Madame, marry him quickly. The fiancée isn't far away, damn it, and I'm sure that she's dreaming about the marriage—isn't that so, girl?"

With that, a confused smile and blush on the part of Louisette. And days, and days, of illness, with Maman and my cousin, my head lost in the horror of darkness.

Frightful nights of sleep populated by dreams and nightmares, all my base orgy passing before my eyes again and again; sinister faces: Charlot and his strange androgynous head, Totor and his cut-throat face, the masks of thieves and whores, and the Spider Man, the terrible Spider Man evoked by Totor, his frog-like eyes, his "work," his monstrous red spiders that quit his hand and climb my breast to the throat, bite me and suck my blood avidly, all my blood . . . all . . . all my blood!

Oh, those red spiders, which swell, swell, become enormous, heavy, crushing me with their weight . . .

My sad awakenings, my constrained smiles at my mother and cousin, the relief of finding them again in the morning after my terror at seeing them go away in the evening and leaving me alone, defenseless against the phantoms. How many times have I retained myself in order not to scream my suffering?

My sad awakenings! My days lived in an armchair near the window, and that décor of madness and murder, that Boulevard d'Italie which brings my thoughts back implacably to the evil evenings, the evenings of yesterday, so unhealthy for my soul, the soul of a whore who has partied too much and who offers herself joylessly to the kisses of all, out of habit . . .

XXXIV

AM I alive or dead? Was I dreaming? Have I lived?
I have just found myself again, suddenly, at home, in the normal world, in the light of pink candles, in front of the mirror in my dressing-room.

Is it me? Is that really me in there?

And I consider myself curiously, like a stranger. How these last six months of complete madness and hallucination have ravaged me! Let's see, is it me, that face, over which a disquieting smile is fluttering, that face with the pallor of old ivory? And in those blue-gray eyes, ordinarily veiled, in those distant eyes, is that suffocating and empty gaze of the dead pupils really mine? And those Japanese hands, those slender hands, splayed and then closed like hairy chrysanthemums, are they mine, those continually twitching alcoholic hands?

For a fortnight, Morphine has conquered me. La Morphine! It alone illuminates my thought and my life momentarily, it alone makes the world around me crepitate with an artificial intensity, the world that appears to me to be subjugated, even by day, by a frightful twilight. Thanks to her, here I am, re-entered into the new life; yes, in truth. I have re-entered by interversion into a sphere of hallucination, like a being awakening abruptly. It's thanks to her, whom I retain within me, in the domain of golden dreams, that you no longer encounter in nocturnal Paris the gentleman dressed like you, with the ironic speech, the cruel words, the young man with too many pearl and ruby rings, in whose presence so many people seem disquieted, by I know not what indefinable difference that naturally gives birth on their lips to the word "strange."

La Morphine! Yes, it's thanks to her that I'm no longer

> *the haunter of the suburbs and Sunday ballrooms,*
> *The equivocal prowler of culpable amours,*

the sad hero of so many evil legends, a man whom hooligans address familiarly, and whom demoiselles of random amour are glad to see: the young man who will be found one day cut to pieces on the river bank at Billancourt or in the waste ground at Grenelle, "which so often served Odette de Lavallière."[1] La Morphine. Yes, it's thanks to her that I can finally see myself.

But now, a delectable crystalline voice emerges from the mirror and responds to me:

"Undoubtedly you're still alive, or, more accurately, simulating life. But why delude yourself with words? You're alive! Let me laugh! Are you quite sure you're alive?

---

1 This fictitious name, presumably adopted by a prostitute, combines those of Odette de Champdivers, the chief mistress of Charles VI, and Louise de La Vallière, one of the chief mistresses of Louis XIV.

You think you're saved from the arms of Arachne? Child! Are you forgetting, then, that I never quit my lovers, my mistresses . . . I always hold them . . . You haven't reconquered yourself. Remember that you're nothing but a grotesque and unusual appearance of a man, a curious automaton with movements sufficiently opportune and conventional for unobservant minds. But reflect carefully as to whether you resemble those people who go forth without knowing where, saluting and grimacing a smile mechanically. You can longer, now, move, speak and smile of your own accord . . . *you're empty* . . . All your sensations, all your sentiments and desires, I have caused to descend from the living degree, from the vital point, beneath which is the point of indifference. You are no longer anything but a rag devoid of a name in the language, a phantom unreality . . . and still my plaything!"

And the voice laughs, and laughs . . . Frightened, I lean toward the mirror, against the pitted glass. And it is Her that I see, Her, the Phantom. I recognize her hallucinatory mask of a Strix, her inverted triangular head, her skin as if impregnated with sandalwood, holed by eyes that are not sad this time, but the true eyes of a laughing houri, so shiny that one might think them enameled.

The mask animates . . .

Oh yes, it's really Her, the Phantom. Her and her errant soul; her and her nightmare head glimpsed for a long time in hours of ether, the flower of vice and sad sensuality . . . Her! And her head resembles that of Charlot, *Monsieur Polaire* . . .

And now a smile parts her mouth, in which radiantly white teeth appear . . . and then, instinctively, I recoil, afraid of being bitten while the face lights up, ignited like a bowl of punch . . . Now it vanishes. In its place, the reflection shows itself in the looking-glass as a red hand, a gigantic hand . . . It leaps from the frame on to the carpet . . . It bounds, crawls, stretches itself and runs like a spider, hectically . . .

Meanwhile, the crystalline voice whispers in my ear:

> *I have eaten from the tambour and drunk from the cymbal,*
> *And I have eaten your heart and drunk your brain . . .*[1]

---

1 The first line of this couplet is taken from a plaque allegedly related to the Eleusinian Mysteries; it had been quoted by Gérard de Nerval in "Sylvie" (1853)

XXXV

"ANDHRÉ, my child, be reasonable... begging you to obey her... Get married... let me marry you..."

The scene of this afternoon, a few hours ago. Maman beside me, Maman almost sobbing, Maman truly, and for the first time, "my mother." She put her arms around me, hugged me and petted me, and I thought I had become very small again, a small child. I had a six-year-old soul; I wept... and my tears were so sweet, so sweet!

Twenty years of solitude, hostility and anxiety flowed in my tears; all of my sad and concentrated life between my starting school and the day when I collapsed, unconscious. It was like the extirpation of a cancer that had been eating me away for a long time, the thrust of the scalpel into the pocket of bile that was hooked on to my heart. Twenty years of unhappiness flowed out of me, trickling in my sweet, warm tears... And Maman's voice, an unknown voice, a forgotten voice, a motherly voice, catechized me.

"Marry, my Andhré, marry.[1] It's your life, and mine,

---

[1] When Jean Lorrain moved to Auteuil from his apartment in the "haunted house" where he suffered the hallucinations that he mined for inspiration in his "*contes d'un buveur d'éther*" he invited his wid-

that depend on that marriage . . . and Louisette loves you so much! She will be the sweet and loving wife that you need. She will preserve you from the follies of life—because, my poor child, you have such a weak character, You're truly effeminate, my Andhré, and Louisette will be like a very attentive big sister for you—even better, like a very reasonable big brother."

And Maman smiled through her tears; and I accepted: I shall marry in a month.

Oh, why did I not confess to my mother just now, why did I not tell her about my anguish, my haunting . . . why, why? She would have suffered. Wouldn't her suffering have been almost legitimate? For the tyranny of my nightmares is partly her fault. What human being could resist twenty years of abandonment?

Come on, let's calm down. The bad dreams are definitively buried in the past. Marriage will make me a different man. And I want that. In the depths of the alcove we can be two, strictly speaking, to defend me against the phantom . . .

---

owed mother to live with him, and she subsequently moved with him to Nice, remaining with him until his death. There is, of course, no record of their relationship or her attitude to his lifestyle or his sexuality.

XXXVI

WE can be two, to defend me against the phantom, I wrote, three evenings ago in these notes, which are the reflections of my life and my sickness.

Stupidity! Louisette will never understand me. Certainly, she is sweet, maternal even. She is the wife that I need, the wife chosen for me by my mother. I am sure that she will not fail in the task of devotion imposed upon her. Perhaps she loves me, amorously . . . who can tell?

For myself, I don't love her. Everything about her distances me from her: her laughter and her candid eyes, the grace that flowers in her mouth, everything, everything . . . I'm allowing myself to be married to please Maman, and I sense very clearly that I am going to enchain my life very stupidly.

What I need is a wife whose soul is as ravaged as mine, whose veins are full of mud. Next to someone like that, I would be better off than with a defender against the Phantom; I would have found an accomplice, we could both have sought, in the worst depravities and the most equivocal adventures, the forgetfulness of my madness.

For I can see madness coming; it is at the end of the road that I am descending. Oh, the wife that I need! A Messalina aggravated by the strange and avid for the unprecedented. But instead of that flower of evil, I'm plucking a lily . . .

Yesterday, again, I had the clear sensation of everything that separates us, Louisette and me.

We were going shopping, alone, like two lovers, looking for agreeable furnishing fabrics, saffron velvets in slightly dead tones, with which we planned to have curtains made for the bedroom—the nuptial chamber about which I cannot think without sardonic laughter rising to my lips.

Before us, the salesmen displayed samples, showing off the fabrics, and Louisette, indecisive, asked for other shades of the same color. I refrained from touching the fabrics; the sensation of velvet has always put me into an indescribable state of nervousness, and I have never been able to touch women dressed in velvet, or even brush past workers in the street wearing trousers in that cloth, without feeling a complicated malaise, a malaise that makes my flesh shudder with joy and pain at the same time.

So, Louisette was requesting other shades when, suddenly perceiving a piece placed to one side, of oxblood red, she exclaimed: "Show me that one; that's the one I want." And, turning toward me "What if we take that red?"

At the same time she handed me an end of the unfolded cloth, inviting me to touch the velvet.

Oh, that impression! I was dazzled, veritably dazzled. A host of unformulated desires rose up within me . . . it was like a thirst for joyful cruelty that dried my throat, a need to do something evil that drove me to take my cousin's hand and squeeze it like a vice...

She uttered an exclamation "Andhré, you're hurting me!"

I relaxed my grip and, panicked, ran out of the shop. The Phantom had woken up again, for a second.

When she caught up with me on the edge of the sidewalk, outside the door, I had calmed down. Crestfallen, I was about to apologize, to invent a malaise... when, in the most natural voice in the world and a tone of mild reproach she said: "Naughty! What must the employees have thought?"

She thought that my grip was evidence of amour!

Am I not right to say that I am making the most absurd marriage possible? And that for human respect, because I dare not confess my sickness! Oh, that Louisette, who, when she arrived in the house, gave the impression of understanding me, to whom, six months ago, I was sympathetic... how I hate her now!

XXXVII

IT'S over! The Phantom is victorious.
Oh, that red spider!
It was yesterday, in the afternoon. The rain was beating its incessant reveille on the windows.

After lunch, in the drawing room, Maman reminded me of some of my childhood memories, certain parties given for the children of officers garrisoned in Oran when my father was commanding his zouaves. And I too, in a corner of my memory, had rediscovered a glimmer of that time. Gradually, with Maman's aid, a scene was disengaged: a children's ball was resuscitated. I saw myself again in my costume of a little zouzou, grave and solemn, in order to copy Papa. That was it . . . I recognized the scamp who, having heard the Mexican campaign narrated so many times and the battle of Santonio in which my father, with thirty-four men, held out for three days against fifteen hundred enemies,[1] loudly criticizing the little comrades whose parents had only hired the costumes of

---

1 There was no such battle during the French invasion of Mexico (1862-1867).

Pierrots or Columbines. I had the very militaristic sentiment that the uniform trumps civilian dress.

Suddenly, my mother declared: "Your little zouzou costume must still exist, Andhré. It's in a trunk in the loft, with the trinkets and clothes that we brought back from Algeria when your father retired. One day, after your marriage, my children, we must go up into that loft. Seeing all those old things will distract us."

That same evening, yesterday evening, after Maman had retired to her room, Louisette and I plotted to go and look around up there under the eaves. My cousin had accepted my plan with enthusiasm.

Oh, that loft! I only climbed up there very rarely, and when we went into it the tremulous light of our candles displayed a décor that, in my own house, was entirely strange to me. After a few minutes, however, I began to recognize things: furniture, including old armchairs and dressers, that had garnished one room or another in the time when my grandmother lived alone in the house. And other memories of youth surged forth: one leather-clad armchair, rickety, worm-eaten and useless today, I had once had in my present bedroom. Grandmother had been particularly fond of it and would not let anyone sit on it . . . But what attracted me most were the trunks, the big trunks that we had brought back from Algeria, one of which must contain the zouzou costume, that souvenir of my childhood, which hallucinated me, which I wanted to see again at any price, and without delay. The first trunk was eviscerated; its contents, shifted by me, revealed nothing. It was the same with the second. But the third . . . scarcely had I lifted the lid than the red trousers and the little jacket were before my eyes.

I seized it, the little jacket, with agitated hands . . . an indescribable emotion had gripped me . . . my eyes filled with tears, large tears . . . it seemed to me that my heart was about to burst in my breast . . .

Oh, that moment of perfect happiness, that innocent and candid happiness, and that sensation of deliverance, that innocent past, which chased away the Phantom of the black past!

"Oh, Andhré . . . Andhré! Throw it away! Throw it away!"

I dropped the little jacket . . . and I perceived, running over it, an enormous red spider, a terrible spider, as large as a small crab . . .

It was only a momentary vision, which scarcely lasted a second, but Louisette dropped the candle and became crazed by panic, fear having possessed her; and I fled behind her, stumbling like a drunkard . . .

XXXVIII

I couldn't sleep. I could still see it, the hideous beast. It was really her—it was more than her: it was the grim divinity of the Obsession, it was Arachne: Arachne, the hideous goddess who has been torturing me for months, Arachne, the perfidious spinner, who gorges herself on blood, the horrible ghoul who holds all under her charm and bewitches all madmen, all those fascinated by Obsession, all the men like the exhibitor of spiders and me. What duplicity has she not employed in order to seize me, how many hours of panic has she not exacerbated in me, how many steps and countersteps has she not made me execute; in what labyrinths has she not lost me!

All that madness, all that anguish, those solitary amusements at Noyon and elsewhere, those joyful terrors before the quivering hands of whores, those excursions on the river bank, those infatuations with flowers, those days of crapulous pleasure: all of that to trap me, to absorb me . . .

And it's my childhood, the white Phantom of my childhood, that has been her accomplice, which brought me back to the loft and sent me in search of the monstrous spider, the red spider . . .

Her body full of bloody pus, her legs short and hairy, she is living in a crease in my infantile disguise. I have never seen her like. She must come from the Bièvre, which accumulates its filth at the very foot of our house, this old town house, once placed, at the time of its erection, in the most charming of landscapes, now surrounded by ignoble tanneries.

Yes, she must come from the Bièvre. It's on the banks of that miry stream, in which hides corroded by putrefaction sicken, that she has lived, and lives . . .

XXXIX

ANOTHER week eaten by Her: Her, the Red Spider. And in a week, I'm getting married. It's the end. I'm finished, finished. I'm running toward incoherence. The notation of my anguish on this paper, the notation that calmed me slightly, is now a torture. Madness is approaching; I sense it. My God, what have I become?

Every day, while Maman and Louisette are busy with preparations for the marriage, furtively, like a thief, I slip into the loft and I stay there, watching for her slightest movement. She has conquered me, conquered me completely. Her desires have become my desires . . . she's within me . . .

And I hate her. I can't, however, kill her, for she's stronger than I am. She dominates me. I can see the day coming when I shall offer her my blood, in order that she can get drunk on my life . . .

It's the end.

XL

WHAT a scandal, and what must people be thinking!

Just now, in the sacristy, after mass, seeing all those gloved hands extended toward us, the married couple, a madness rose in my brain . . . Oh, all those hands, all those clawed paws! I shoved everyone out of the way and I fled . . .

Outside, it was raining, the sky weeping, the horizon low. I leapt into a carriage and hurled an address at the coachman—and what an address! The name of a riverside dive resurfaced in my memory abruptly: the *Clown de l'Hippodrome* on the Quai de Billancourt; and the carriage rolled, rolled, rolled . . .

A dive, an ignoble dive . . . two plastered whores . . . and the old woman, the old flower-seller, who smiled on seeing me come in . . . and the remarks of the whores, their sniggering, my name whispered, my name in the mouths of that population . . . All the thieves in Paris know one another . . . Charlot, Totor and the rest must have exchanged confidences in my regard. People know me, or believe they know me; ignominious epithets are attached to my name. Misery of my life!

And the old woman smiling there, winking . . . her honeyed voice . . . our exit . . . the place where she brought me . . . that waste ground near the leaden water . . . some thirty caravans, dormant on muddy wheels . . . greasy, filthy soil . . . vermin, mangy dogs, emaciated, one-eyed cats . . . and children, abominable brats.

Oh, the frightful old woman and the little creature, boy or girl that she presented to me . . . the eyes of the child, dark eyes, elongated, as if enlarged by kohl . . . bloody lips in a savage face, the hue of old ivory, tenebrous hair with blue glints . . . and I was perhaps about to . . .

But the little creature agitated its hands—red hands, always red hands—and I was afraid. I ran, ran, ran . . . I ran away, pursued by sniggers, insults, laughter and stones . . .

The day is dying. I daren't return to the house . . . what can I say to Maman? To Louisette . . . my wife?

In this café where I'm scribbling all hands seem to be raised against me, grasping . . . always the hands, the hands, the hands . . .

XLI

HOW dark it is in my poor head! A black and red night, populated with restless hands. What shadow is enveloping me! Why is life crushing me, like an excessively heavy cloak? By what mystery are those hands that are dancing around me "knitting" like that with their paws . . . the hairy legs of the red spider?

I returned to the house. With what alarm old Yves, who preceded me, candle in hand, through the corridors of our dwelling, looked at me!

When I stopped outside the door of our room, when he saw me turn the doorknob, he put the candle-tray on the ground precipitately and fled uttering cries of horror . . .

Louisette was there. It's Her who wanted to see me first, in order to spare me Maman's interrogations on the subject of my fit of madness this morning, in the sacristy. She, she alone, wanted to confess me . . .

I smiled on perceiving her; I smiled as I listened to her . . . the looking-glass sent back my image. I had never seen a living being more similar to me. No, never more fear in a dry gaze . . .

She chatted . . .

I sensed that something was going awry in my head.

She chatted, interrogating me . . . but what could she get out of me? I muttered inconsequential words . . .

My thought populated the room with hands that were still shaking, seeking to grasp something, grabbing and convulsive hands, blind hands that only found emptiness . . . madly hairy chrysanthemums, enormous dahlias—arachnid dahlias—born, running, vanishing, to be reborn, again and forever . . . as if I were in an opium and ether dream, and an alexandrine, always the same, obsessed me:

Poisons I've absorbed are giving me a headache . . .

Oh, I can feel something going awry . . .

Louisette must have understood that I was going mad, but . . .

By a sublime effort, she made the smile flourish in her eyes again, bringing back the phantom of amour. God! How healthy she was, how fresh her flesh was! With what frenzy I enlaced her, how I crushed my mouth on hers, how I sucked in her breath!

Desperation! My lips agitated in sterile and empty kisses. From my heart, whose beating I could hear, nothing sprang but fear . . . an atrocious fear . . . sobs of madness, desperation and impotence creaking in my breast, rising into my throat, choking me . . .

Louisette!

She enveloped me with her embrace and hugged me wildly . . . I shuddered in her arms . . . All my pain filtered slowly, like an inexhaustible spring, relentlessly, through my kisses, my bites, my feigned smiles . . .

What darkness thickened within me!

The room was carpeted in red. The very low and very broad bed was all draped with red velvet, heightened by arachnean lace of mourning . . .

Mechanically, she undressed . . .

And turbulently, hands and flowers were still dancing around me . . . I was animating them . . . an insipid odor of blood was floating in the room . . .

Something, nothing . . . I was sure now and I was laughing at it . . . stretched out and went awry in my brain . . .

Louisette was half-naked, slightly anxious, and looking at me . . .

Hands and red flowers stained the darkness in places . . . clawed forms mingled with their dances . . .

Madly, I quit the room and went up to the loft.

The hands and the flowers were still pursuing me. The clawed forms were swarming. All the hands and all the flowers and all the monsters were exchanging eyes of sardonyx and opal.

I opened the trunk. I took out the zouzou costume . . . the costume in a crease of which the red spider was lying in ambush. The beast was swollen . . .

I returned to the bedroom.

The hands, the flowers and the forms that had only followed me until then ran around Louisette. I saw the little velvet hands, atrociously red, with carp-like leaps, climbing up her legs to her thighs . . .

I stammered a few words, disorderly phrases . . .

The Red Spider! I wanted to place it on Louisette. I wanted it to climb her legs as well, to the thighs . . . I begged her, I threatened her with kisses, with passionate words . . .

Her eyes opened immeasurably, enlarged like abysses . . . and I was able to contemplate, suspended over those vertiginous depths, all the Empyreum of fear . . .

Her hands were knitting too . . . Oh, those hands, which were dancing, contorting, elongating and clenching, and opening again . . . her mad hands, clawing at the void . . .

She refused herself to my passion. Her mouth grimaced with horror. She tried to scream. She couldn't. Hoarse breath escaped between her lips. Her teeth clicked.

And the hands, the hands that were still beating the air . . .

And the red spider that was running over the bed . . . over my hands . . . the red spider that had caught me . . . and to which Louisette did not want to give herself . . .

An explosion ripped apart my human reason. Louisette burst out in strident and prolonged laughter . . . the poor laughter of a madwoman, a laughter of fear . . . and I too was afraid . . . afraid of Maman, who might wake up, afraid of the domestics who might come running, afraid of Louisette's laughter, afraid of everything . . . and afraid of myself . . .

My hands were *knitting* in their turn, my hands rose to her throat, convulsed, squeezed, squeezed . . .

And the red spider ran over the red bed in the red room . . .

※

Where am I going in my profound night? I'm running, running, ever more quickly, ever more quickly . . . The hands, the flowers, the forms are whirling . . . It's rising to my throat, it's strangling me. I'm running, running . . .

The beast is in my head. It's knitting, knitting feverishly, always at the same point of the same thought. It's running behind my forehead, in my nerves, in my blood . . .

It's Her . . . HER . . .

※

Thus conclude the notes bequeathed to me by poor Andhré Mordann.

What has become of the poor fellow? And his family? His mother? Did he really strangle his young wife?

As many problems that I can't resolve. At any rate, the frightful crime of which he accuses himself has never been revealed to the public. But one should not hasten to take from that a negative response. Many murders of which one never hears mention are committed in Paris and elsewhere. Who can tell whether, out of regard for the family, for the name of the murderer, given the pointlessness of pursuits to be exercised against a poor madman, human justice has not kept silent about that frightful tragedy? The press only knows about crimes of that genre what the police want to reveal.

The Breton box is still there before me, concealing its yellowed papers. Sometimes, when I am ready to allow myself to attempt something impossible, to seek to refine impressions, the sight of it is salutary for me.

Yes, let us sometimes dream of unachievable paintings and books, of rare sensations, but let us beware of the Absolute, which is always in our shadow and is always extending its arms to us . . .

APPENDIX

THE DEDICATION

TO JEAN LORRAIN

I am dedicating this somber story to you, my dear Jean, because I love your talent and your amity. And have I not also to thank you for having equipped this journal of madness and death with the works that mark it in literary history. This is what you wrote a few weeks ago in one of your *Joies de Paris* in *Le Journal*:[1]

"The waste ground! An essentially Parisian landscape, which found its chronicler in Joris-Karl Huysmans and its painter in Raffaëlli, in the most magisterial pages that the author of *À rebours* has ever consecrated to the sparse grass and flowers of the shards of oyster-shells and old sardine-tins comprising that Eden of detritus:

---

1 The quoted article appeared in the issue of *Le Journal* for 30 September 1901, referring to areas of ground marked by the municipal council for future development but fenced off in the meantime, which became favorite refuges for amorous rendezvous. If the reference to "a few weeks" can be taken seriously it implies that the novel must have been completed before the end of 1901, although it was not published until February 1903.

an entire literary school has even been created around that field of filth. Lucien Descaves, in *Sous-Off*, Jean Ajalbert in *Sur le Talus*, Oscar Méténier in *Madame la Boule*[1] and Delphi Fabrice, in *L'Araignée rouge*, have, in their turn, loved, described, depicted and detailed amorously that essentially Parisian wart, that wound exposed by Joris-Karl Huysmans in *Les Soeurs Vatard* and *La Fille Elisa*. Edmond de Goncourt had perhaps explored it before him. What am I saying? The waste ground is even Romantic. It is in the waste ground of the Barrière d'Italie that Victor Hugo situates the inn to which the Thénardiers try to draw Fantine's adoptive father, the former Monsieur Madeleine and the authentic Jean Valjean, for whom Javert is lying in wait, and who is saved by Marius. The waste ground even plays a role in the tales of Théodore de Banville, the most chimerical of poets, and Catulle Mendès, in his *Maison de la Vieille*, does not disdain to frame a curious idyll there. I shall not mention the songs of Bruant. of which the waste ground is the habitual terrain, marvelously composed for the pencil of Steinlen . . ."

My name mingled with those illustrious names: that is the glory that has fallen to me before its time. How will my novel live up to that aureole, if I dare put it thus?

---

1 Lucien Descaves' *Sous-Offs* (1889) escaped conviction on a charge of offending the army, but the author was stripped of his military rank. Jean Ajalbert, the author of the poem *Sur le talus* (book 1887) also ran into trouble with the law as an outspoken polemicist for Anarchist and Dreyfusard causes. Oscar Méténier's play *Mademoiselle Fifi*, based on a Guy de Maupassant short story, was initially banned by the censor before causing a sensation at the Grand-Guignol; *Madame la Boule* was first published in 1890.

And since you have had the imprudence to cite *L'Araignée rouge*, it is necessary that you hear part of its history and one of its avatars, for it has had avatars.

It came into the world in two forms, in a play and novel. In a play, it was incarnated by one of our friends in the strange figure of a strix; it emerged on to the boards in a disquieting décor, summoned to offer error to the audience . . . and Monsieur Roujon passed by, who eliminated it from the world with a stroke of his blue pencil.[1]

Oh, my dear Jean, can you imagine the day when Monsieur Roujon killed my play? That was accomplished in the Rue de Valois, in the directorial office. I was accompanied there by a député, for I had remembered this advice of our Méténier: "When one has dealings with the Censor, it is always necessary to go to see the minister or the director of the Beaux-Arts with a député or a senator." I had, therefore, asked a friend who is a député to escort me. On the way I had found convincing arguments—or what I believed to be such—in order to persuade Monsieur Roujon to let my play live, but I had reckoned without my député. No sooner had we been introduced into His Excellency's study than my député started braying: "Citizen Roujon, it would be wrong to ban Delphi Fabrice's play because . . ." Monsieur Roujon

---

1 The former managing editor of one of the periodicals founded by Catulle Mendès, Henry Roujon (1853-1914) became Director of the French Ministry of Fine Arts in 1894. He was named permanent secretary of the Académie des Beaux-Arts in 1904 and was elected as a member of the Académie Française in 1911. When Fabrice wrote this he could not know that he and Jean Lorrain would be embroiled in a long battle with Roujon in the last months of 1904 to persuade him not to censor their play *Clair de Lune*.

stood up, made a sign to the office boy, who had not yet gone out, and, addressing my friend, he pronounced: "Monsieur, when you want to employ less parliamentary language, I will listen to you . . ." And we left, my friend still braying, talking about social revolution, the budget, the Commune, etc., while I turned my white hat—it was summer in the middle of the Exposition.

And my play was buried. My friend promised that he would say a few words about the matter to the minister but a député's promises . . . Oh, my dear Jean, if you ever have difficulties with the Censor, believe me, don't embarrass yourself with a representative of the people!

I have related this adventure to you in order to make you smile—and it pleases me to make you smile, if possible, before the beginning of this black, black, black tale . . .

My hands,
D.F.

A PARTIAL LIST OF SNUGGLY BOOKS

G. ALBERT AURIER *Elsewhere and Other Stories*
CHARLES BARBARA *My Lunatic Asylum*
S. HENRY BERTHOUD *Misanthropic Tales*
LÉON BLOY *The Desperate Man*
LÉON BLOY *The Tarantulas' Parlor and Other Unkind Tales*
ÉLÉMIR BOURGES *The Twilight of the Gods*
BERNARDO CUOTO CASTILLO *Asphodels*
CYRIEL BUYSSE *The Aunts*
JAMES CHAMPAGNE *Harlem Smoke*
FÉLICIEN CHAMPSAUR *The Latin Orgy*
BRENDAN CONNELL *Clark*
BRENDAN CONNELL *Unofficial History of Pi Wei*
RAFAELA CONTRERAS *The Turquoise Ring and Other Stories*
ADOLFO COUVE *When I Think of My Missing Head*
QUENTIN S. CRISP *Aiaigasa*
LADY DILKE *The Outcast Spirit and Other Stories*
CATHERINE DOUSTEYSSIER-KHOZE *The Beauty of the Death Cap*
ÉDOUARD DUJARDIN *Hauntings*
BERIT ELLINGSEN *Now We Can See the Moon*
ERCKMANN-CHATRIAN *A Malediction*
ENRIQUE GÓMEZ CARRILLO *Sentimental Stories*
EDMOND AND JULES DE GONCOURT *Manette Salomon*
REMY DE GOURMONT *From a Faraway Land*
GUIDO GOZZANO *Alcina and Other Stories*
EDWARD HERON-ALLEN *The Complete Shorter Fiction*
RHYS HUGHES *Cloud Farming in Wales*
J.-K. HUYSMANS *The Crowds of Lourdes*
J.-K. HUYSMANS *Knapsacks*
COLIN INSOLE *Valerie and Other Stories*
JUSTIN ISIS *Pleasant Tales II*
JUSTIN ISIS AND DANIEL CORRICK (editors)
    Drowning in Beauty: The Neo-Decadent Anthology

VICTOR JOLY *The Unknown Collaborator and Other Legendary Tales*
MARIE KRYSINSKA *The Path of Amour*
BERNARD LAZARE *The Mirror of Legends*
BERNARD LAZARE *The Torch-Bearers*
MAURICE LEVEL *The Shadow*
JEAN LORRAIN *Errant Vice*
JEAN LORRAIN *Fards and Poisons*
JEAN LORRAIN *Masks in the Tapestry*
JEAN LORRAIN *Nightmares of an Ether-Drinker*
JEAN LORRAIN *The Soul-Drinker and Other Decadent Fantasies*
GEORGES DE LYS *An Idyll in Sodom*
ARTHUR MACHEN *N*
ARTHUR MACHEN *Ornaments in Jade*
CAMILLE MAUCLAIR *The Frail Soul and Other Stories*
CATULLE MENDÈS *Bluebirds*
CATULLE MENDÈS *For Reading in the Bath*
CATULLE MENDÈS *Mephistophela*
ÉPHRAÏM MIKHAËL *Halyartes and Other Poems in Prose*
LUIS DE MIRANDA *Who Killed the Poet?*
OCTAVE MIRBEAU *The Death of Balzac*
CHARLES MORICE *Babels, Balloons and Innocent Eyes*
DAMIAN MURPHY *Daughters of Apostasy*
KRISTINE ONG MUSLIM *Butterfly Dream*
CHARLES NODIER *Outlaws and Sorrows*
PHILOTHÉE O'NEDDY *The Enchanted Ring*
YARROW PAISLEY *Mendicant City*
URSULA PFLUG *Down From*
JEREMY REED *When a Girl Loves a Girl*
ADOLPHE RETTÉ *Misty Thule*
JEAN RICHEPIN *The Bull-Man and the Grasshopper*
DAVID RIX *A Blast of Hunters*
FREDERICK ROLFE (Baron Corvo) *Amico di Sandro*
FREDERICK ROLFE (Baron Corvo)
   An Ossuary of the North Lagoon and Other Stories

JASON ROLFE *An Archive of Human Nonsense*
ARNAUD RYKNER *The Last Train*
MARCEL SCHWOB *The Assassins and Other Stories*
MARCEL SCHWOB *Double Heart*
CHRISTIAN HEINRICH SPIESS *The Dwarf of Westerbourg*
BRIAN STABLEFORD (editor)
   Decadence and Symbolism: A Showcase Anthology
BRIAN STABLEFORD (editor) *The Snuggly Satyricon*
BRIAN STABLEFORD *The Insubstantial Pageant*
BRIAN STABLEFORD *Spirits of the Vasty Deep*
BRIAN STABLEFORD *The Truths of Darkness*
COUNT ERIC STENBOCK *Love, Sleep & Dreams*
COUNT ERIC STENBOCK *Myrtle, Rue & Cypress*
COUNT ERIC STENBOCK *The Shadow of Death*
COUNT ERIC STENBOCK *Studies of Death*
MONTAGUE SUMMERS *The Bride of Christ and Other Fictions*
MONTAGUE SUMMERS *Six Ghost Stories*
GILBERT-AUGUSTIN THIERRY *The Blonde Tress and The Mask*
GILBERT-AUGUSTIN THIERRY *Reincarnation and Redemption*
DOUGLAS THOMPSON *The Fallen West*
TOADHOUSE *Gone Fishing with Samy Rosenstock*
TOADHOUSE *Living and Dying in a Mind Field*
RUGGERO VASARI *Raun*
JANE DE LA VAUDÈRE *The Demi-Sexes and The Androgynes*
JANE DE LA VAUDÈRE *The Priestesses of Mylitta*
JANE DE LA VAUDÈRE *Syta's Harem and Pharaoh's Lover*
AUGUSTE VILLIERS DE L'ISLE-ADAM *Isis*
RENÉE VIVIEN AND HÉLÈNE DE ZUYLEN DE NYEVELT
   Faustina and Other Stories
RENÉE VIVIEN *Lilith's Legacy*
RENÉE VIVIEN *A Woman Appeared to Me*
TERESA WILMS MONTT *In the Stillness of Marble*
TERESA WILMS MONTT *Sentimental Doubts*
KAREL VAN DE WOESTIJNE *The Dying Peasant*